Murder at the Island Spa

Sharon McGregor

Whimsical Publications, LLC

Florida

Murder at the Island Spa is a work of fiction. Names, characters, and incidents are the products of the author's imagination and are either fictitious or are used fictitiously. Any resemblance to actual events or persons, living or dead, is entirely coincidental.

To purchase the authorized electronic edition of *Murder at the Island Spa*, visit
www.whimsicalpublications.com

Cover art by Traci Markou
Editing by Destiny Booze

ISBN-13: 978-1-940707-41-9

Published by
Whimsical Publications, LLC
Florida

"I was never bored with you, Abby." Richard leaned over and touched her hand.

Abby moved away. "Let's not go there. I better get back and make my getaway plans. Ajax isn't going to like being left with a minder."

"You still have that cat? He must be getting on now."

"He is, but so am I." She knew Richard was about to make some gallant speech about her not aging, but she could do without his platitudes and quickly said, "Don't say it." She stood up. "I'm off then. I do hope you and Kelly have a great Christmas."

"You too."

She felt his eyes on her back as she left. Richard could usually tell what she was thinking, but she had never quite plumbed the depths of his mind, even after all these years. In spite of his seemingly open, outgoing and rather charismatic personality, he kept a part of himself unrevealed, even to his wife of over twenty years.

Back at home, Abby tackled her wardrobe problems. She could do with a quick shopping excursion, she thought, but there weren't too many shops that carried summer stock in December. So she'd have to make do. She tried on all her last year's shorts and tops as well as a couple of dressier outfits. They fit a little more snugly than they did a year ago, but as she turned in the mirror, it didn't seem to show. If she could keep on the straight and narrow diet-wise till she left, these should work okay.

Neil called her the moment he heard she was able to join him on the trip to Turks and Caicos. He offered to pick her up at the airport. He was going to get there a day before she did. The sound of his voice distracted her from Matthew's absence and thoughts of missing her family during Christmas.

Abby arranged for her next door neighbor to look after Ajax and check her plants and mail while she was gone. She felt a little lost for the next week and a half, waiting for her holiday, unable to concentrate on work where she freelanced in the field of education, writing instruction programs and textbooks. She was between projects at the moment, so nothing was pressing. The rest of the world was buying turkeys, making pumpkin pies and mincemeat tarts, and baking shortbread, but, this year, she could pass on all that.

She put her tree up and decorated it, the old tree she and Richard had used for years. It stood in the corner of the living room just to the side of the big window. This would be the third Christmas since their divorce. She had kept the house when they had split. Mandy had still lived at home then, so Abby had tried to keep everything the same as it always had been—the same furniture, the same traditions, the same habits. Now, maybe it was time for a change. When the holidays were over, she would redecorate. She gave a little shudder at the thought of parting with a big slice of her life, but they were just furnishings, just objects. The memories, she would keep.

Not knowing Mandy's plans or timing, she trimmed the tree on her own. When the kids were little, it had always been Mandy's job to put the angel on the top, lifted by her brother. Abby had always liked having the tree up early. She loved the Christmas feeling and wanted it to start as soon as possible. On the other hand, she always took the decorations down as soon as Christmas was over. When it was done, it was done. She resolved to do something similar with her life now. Richard was gone, she had her own relationship, and it was time to move out of the past. Maybe she would hire a decorator instead of relying on her own ideas. Heaven knew her style was haphazard at best. Left to her own devices, she'd probably end up with different furniture, but the same style, and that's not what she wanted, not what she needed.

She spent some time catching up on her correspondence. There weren't too many Christmas cards this year. Not the number she used to get when she and Richard were married. It seemed they had split their friends just like they had split their assets, and their divorce had been amicable by most standards. A lot of people didn't bother with cards. They sent long e-mail greetings or e-cards nowadays. Abby hated those. They had no personality. On the other hand, she still got her yearly cards packed with long letters from her old college friends, and she loved them. She'd long ago sent hers out.

It was two days before her scheduled flight when she got the call from Mandy.

"Mom?" Her voice was shaky and uncharacteristically soft.

Icy tentacles crept down Abby's spine, her "mother's intuition" sending off warning alarms. "What is it, Mandy? What's wrong?"

"Kelly's dead, Mom. The police were here, and they think someone killed her. They have Dad at the station asking him questions. You have to come."

Acknowledgement

To my daughter Heather who keeps treating me to spas,
but luckily not to ones as deadly as this.

Cast of Characters

The Addisons

Abby Addison—Never says no to a cry for help.
Richard Addison—Abby's ex-husband who has left her for greener pastures.
Kelly—The greener pastures.
Mandy—Richard and Abby's daughter, training to be a veterinarian.
Matthew—Richard and Abby's son who spends most of his time in the hot spots of the world.

The Davenports

Sylvia—The matriarch, recently freed by the death of her husband, Edward, to follow her own pursuits.
Mona—Sylvia's daughter and a chip off her father, Edward's, old block.
Belinda—Sylvia's youngest daughter. She sees things that others don't.
Arthur—As Sylvia's brother, he's not really a Davenport, but he's stepped nicely into his deceased brother-in-law's shoes as the family bully.
Jessie—Arthur's granddaughter and Sylvia's great-niece. Her unwavering loyalty is to her Great-Aunt Sylvia, "Gran."

Island Spa Staff

Stephanie—The manicurist who has eyes for Theo.
Theo—The massage therapist who only has eyes for himself.
Tillie—The gift shop manager, free with information, but how much malice is behind that information?

Chapter One

Abby swiped the last piece of chocolate trifle from her plate and sighed. She could feel the material of her denim skirt stretching to its outer limits. She was going to have to do something about her expanding girth, but the weeks leading up to Christmas were not the best time to be making food resolutions. For now, she pushed herself back slightly from the huge oak dining table as unobtrusively as possible and squirmed in her chair to adjust the way her waistband sat at her midriff.

She looked at her son across the table. "Happy Birthday, Matthew."

"And an early Merry Christmas to you, Mom," he responded with a wide and satisfied smile. Then he sobered. "I'm sorry," he said, "and that goes to you all." He waved around the seated gathering. "I know you planned for my birthday party in the summer, and I really wanted to come, but the way things were..." His voice trailed off, but they all knew he was referring to the volatile conditions in the country where he had been working under Doctors Without Borders. "I was hoping to make it for Christmas too, but this was the best time for me to get away."

"What difference does a date make?" asked Richard. "So we're three months late wishing our son a happy birthday and a month early saying Merry Christmas. We get to spend it together, and that's what counts."

Abby silently echoed her ex-husband's speech.

"The dinner was lovely, Kelly," she said to her hostess, Richard's current romance, hoping her compliment didn't sound grudging, "and the chocolate trifle was out of this world."

"Thanks, Abby." Kelly's bright smile gleamed past perfect teeth and dazzling lips. Her hoop earrings dangled little gold reindeer in honor of the season. How did she manage to keep her lipstick so perfect while eating? It was a trick Abby hadn't mastered. She always ended up having to redo and found it easier just to forgo the lipstick at dinners. "I'm so glad you could come. I think it's always wonderful when women connected to the same man can end up being friends."

Abby smiled, giving the expected response, but thought "friends" might have stretched the truth a smidgen. And "connected?" Even though Richard was her ex-husband, they had severed connections with a divorce. Oh sure, they were civil, respected each other, and even attended family functions for the sake of the kids, but "connected?" No way. They had moved on in their own ways. Now Richard had Kelly, and she had Neil. Well, occasionally she had Neil. There were a few drawbacks to a long range relationship, as she was finding out.

She glanced at Richard. The corners of his mouth twitched as he returned her look. He knew exactly what she was thinking. And worse, he found it amusing.

"Did Richard tell you about our Christmas adventure?" asked Kelly.

"No," said Abby. "What sort of adventure?" Was she mean-spirited to believe that smile on Kelly's face was more of a self-satisfied smirk?

"Well, not an adventure, exactly. We're going to spend the week leading up to Christmas at a spa on Vancouver Island. We wanted to do something different than the usual rounds of Christmas parties and dinners. It will be a nice getaway and very romantic."

That was Richard all right—romantic. The only problem was he had never been exclusive where he spread the romance. Abby hoped Kelly wouldn't find out the hard way as she had. But she knew a small part of her brain was hoping for just that and cursed herself for being petty and vindictive.

Oh dear, she thought, *I'm giving the seven deadly sins a workout tonight. Let's see, I've covered gluttony, greed, envy, pride and malice. What's left? I think lust is one.* A quick look at her ex-husband reminded her she still wasn't impervious to his charm, and she blushed. *Great. Now that I'm blushing for no reason, they'll think I'm menopausal.*

Kelly was explaining the offerings of the spa. "It's mostly a traditional spa with all the usual massage and seaweed treatments and things, but the hotel side has weekend or week-long stays as well as day bookings. And it has a few extras." She locked glances with Richard as if cueing him to take up the thread. He just lifted his wineglass in her direction in an unspoken toast. She looked a little miffed at his lack of input but went on. "They have a sort of New Age theme. There's a resident medium who does séances once a week, and they have crystal healing and pyramid therapy and..." She stopped as though she'd run out of words, a rare thing for Kelly. "Well, anyhow, you know what I mean. It has all of that as well as whirlpools, rainforest showers, saunas, and mud baths. It's really unique, and we'll have a lot of fun."

To Abby's ears, Kelly's voice became surprisingly brittle, floundering like she'd lost her way as she talked about the fun. That's the trouble with mixed family get-togethers. You ran a constant threat of putting your foot in your mouth.

"Have you ever had your chart read, Abby? Your astrological chart, I mean."

"No," said Abby. "I even gave up reading my daily horoscope when I realized it applied to about one-twelfth of the rest of the world." She gave a little laugh to soften the statement in case Kelly took offense.

Kelly frowned and Abby wondered if she'd really expected her to give a serious answer. With Kelly, she never knew.

Mandy piped up. "Kelly's really into New Age, Mom. She found a tarot reader that told her some truly amazing things. They say the medium at the spa has had some unusual connections. Dad and Kelly are going to have their fortunes told. Isn't that right, Dad?" She grinned at him in a saucy manner.

Abby's attention spiked. Mandy led the conversation in a way that was unlike her. She didn't usually stir the waters. Normally, she was quite supportive with her parents' new relationships. Abby thought Mandy was quite taken with Kelly, but she sensed something off in her speech. Maybe things weren't as perfect as Kelly and Richard let on. It seemed to be her night for uncharitable thoughts, but then both Richard and Kelly had that effect on her.

Abby sipped her wine slowly. She had limited herself to half of a glass because she had driven there. Matthew was coming home with her for the night, so maybe she could have her full glass of wine and let him drive home. Matthew had never been much of a drinker even in his teen years and was only having ginger ale tonight.

She wished he was staying longer. They hadn't had much time together, and he would be heading back to the other side of the world in a couple of days. Matthew worked with Doctors Without Borders in all corners of the globe, and Abby often worried about his safety. But he loved what he did and felt fulfilled with his work, so how could she argue with his choices?

Now she hoped they could make a move to leave soon. She'd rather have her glass of wine in the comfort of home. She was beginning to feel stifled in the warm room. The heat was suffocating, and she welcomed the thought of the blast of cold she would feel as they stepped out into the December night. And then, too, she wanted some more time with her son, alone, before he left.

Finally, Kelly stood up, straightening her gray pencil skirt that didn't need straightening, and flicked a few blonde tresses from her shoulder with her right hand. "I'm going to brew some coffee," she said. "I think we need some to wash down the sweetness of that trifle." Although Abby noticed she had barely nibbled at her miniscule portion. That's how she kept that trim figure. Abby had never managed that and didn't know if it was worth all the effort to pass up on life's treats. Not that she was chubby. She wasn't in bad shape at all for her age, but compared to Kelly, well, she felt frowzy.

"We'll help clear," said Mandy, starting to stack empty cake plates. Abby followed her example gladly, and in a few minutes the table was bare except for the wineglasses. Kelly removed the lace tablecloth, leaving the glasses sparkling alone on the polished old table. She produced a stack of coasters from the sideboard and slipped them under the glasses.

"Just leave everything in the sinks," said Kelly. "I'll stack the dishwasher later. Let's give Richard and Matthew some guy time together. I'll pour the coffee and we'll have it in the living room along with a girl chat."

Mandy rolled her eyes at Kelly's retreating back, and the look wasn't lost on Abby, who stifled a giggle. It felt like an old English tradition with the gentlemen leaving the ladies in order to enjoy coffee and cigars in the drawing room, except this was the opposite.

The living room had a masculine look with dark leather furniture, light wood side tables, and wall prints of outdoor scenes. A fireplace with a high mantle dominated the room but was unlit. Two tall, silver trophies sat on the mantle, framing a pottery bowl which held golf balls and tees. She remembered the trophies, as they had once sat in her china cabinet. One was for a golf tournament and the other for top real estate salesman of the year. Obviously, Kelly hadn't moved in with Richard yet, thought Abby. If she had, the décor would be a lot different.

This was her first time in Richard's new house. As a real estate agent, it was likely he bought the house as an investment as much as a home. She fully expected the minute he got a good offer, he'd be moving again. She sat up straight, realizing the wall prints weren't all of fishing scenes. There was a triad of pictures on the wall beside the fireplace. She walked over to take a closer look. Two were copies of photos she had—Matthew in his graduation gown and another of Mandy in jeans and a plaid shirt, holding a newborn white-faced red calf, taken during her summer internship with a veterinarian. The third picture made her smile. It wasn't a professional photo, an outdoors shot of the four of them, all smiling, arms entwined, and Bubbles their old Shepherd lying at their feet, looking as though he smiled too. Who had taken the photo? Oh yes, Mike and Eileen, old friends that had joined them on a two-family picnic by the lake. Poor Bubbles was long gone now. What a name for a German Shepherd! The kids had picked it, so Bubbles it was.

Abby was aware she had looked at the pictures too long when Kelly cleared her throat for attention. "I was just asking Mandy," she said, "if she'd asked you what you thought of our Christmas plans?" Abby felt as though she'd missed something. What did their Christmas plans have to do with her?

Mandy was wearing a rather sheepish expression. "I'm sorry, Mom. I haven't had a chance to talk to you yet. Dad and Kelly want me to join them at the spa for a few days and celebrate Christmas with them. I said I'd have to check and see what plans you had first."

Abby felt trapped by Kelly. Somehow she thought maybe Kelly was doing it deliberately but dismissed it as another uncharitable thought. She wanted to spend Christmas with her children. Matthew was going to be halfway around the word again in a couple of days. She hadn't planned anything specific, just counted on a quiet dinner with Mandy. But she would feel as though she were petty if she tried to convince Mandy to spend Christmas with her. After all, her father had as much right to her company during the holiday as she did. And a stay at a luxury spa was certainly more than she was offering.

She forced a smile. "I haven't planned anything in particular, so of course, Mandy, you'll want to have a visit with your father for Christmas. You and I can do something at home for a New Year and Christmas combined bash." She saw a flash of relief on Mandy's face. She had obviously been stewing over how to break it to her. Abby knew it was a constant struggle for children of divorce to please both parents, and Mandy hadn't seen much of her father lately. If Richard and Kelly were serious about their relationship, Mandy likely saw this as a perfect opportunity to get closer to Kelly.

Isn't that what usually happens in divorced families? Compromise and change.

Richard poked his head around the door. "Kelly, do you know where I put that album of old fishing pictures I dug up last week? I want to show them to Matthew."

Kelly followed him out saying, "I think it's in the office somewhere. I'll look. You'll never find it." So maybe she had moved in with Richard after all. Maybe she just hadn't called in the interior decorators yet. Abby would have to ask Mandy, but then why should she care anyhow?

"I'm sorry, Mom," Mandy began as Kelly's bronze stiletto heels clicked on the way out of the room. "I never had the chance to tell you. I don't have to go. I can celebrate with you and see Dad when he gets back."

"Don't be silly. Of course, you're going. You'll have a terrific time and so will we when you get back." She paused. "It might have to wait till after New Year's though."

"Why?"

Abby smiled. "Neil asked me to go with him to Turks and Caicos for a week. Tom and Tracy are going too."

"What did you tell him?"

"I didn't. I said I'd let him know. Now maybe I'll call him and tell him to count me in. You can go off to the spa and not worry about me if I promise not to worry about you. Agreed?"

"Agreed." Then Mandy said slowly, "How are things going with you and Neil? You haven't talked much about him lately."

"There's not much to talk about. It's a long-distance relationship so we don't see much of each other. Nikki usually has him jetting off on business for the family, and I'm not much into flying." Nikki was Neil's boss and Abby's old college friend. Abby had met Neil last year when responding to Nikki's plea—demand might have been a better word—for help.

"Poor Mom. Nearly everywhere you want to go, you have to fly. I wonder where you got your phobia."

"I don't know, but I have no intention of letting it keep me home. An Ativan or a double rum and coke can do wonders for fear of flying."

Abby glanced at the doorway to be sure Kelly wasn't making a reappearance yet and asked, "What sort of a spa is this? It doesn't sound like a run-of-the-mill place. And a resident medium?"

"It's ordinary for the most part. It has the usual things—mud treatments, glacial clays, massages, water therapy, facials, and salons. But it also has the medium and some other options out of the norm."

"And Kelly's into all this stuff?"

"So it seems, but then Kelly has all sorts of interests that disappear when she gets bored, so I imagine this one will too."

"It seems to me she tried Buddhism once?"

"It didn't last. Too restrictive a lifestyle. She was into yoga and meditation about the time she met Dad. I think she still does the yoga. This paranormal interest will likely be gone by the time we come back."

Mandy sounded as though a shot of cynicism was creeping into her young life way too soon. Abby wondered what effect their marital problems had on her kids. Was that what made Mandy sound older than her twenty-one years? Even though she and Richard had stayed together until the kids were adults, the children must have sensed the underlying problems during their growing years. The divorce carried guilt for Abby because of the children. That was why Abby had made herself believe Richard when he said his affair was a one-time thing. By the time there was a third-time thing, Abby had decided enough was enough. That was three years ago. Matthew had been twenty-two then and out on his own. Mandy had been getting ready for college. Abby's self-image had taken a beating, and she'd known she had to end the marriage. The strange thing was that, in spite of his infidelity, Richard had been a perfect husband otherwise. He was good-natured, funny, a hard worker, a good father and took out the garbage without being asked. Maybe that's why, now three years later, they were able to meet as friends.

Now the baton was being passed to Kelly. Abby couldn't quite bring herself to like the woman who seemed to excel at everything that Abby didn't, but an edge of sympathy crept in. For all Kelly's surface confidence, she was a seeker of sorts, which meant something was missing from her life. Was Richard what she was seeking? If she planned to marry him, Abby hoped Richard had learned how to be a faithful husband. Then she chided herself for the feeling of jealousy that crept into her mind at the thought Kelly might succeed where Abby had failed.

Her thoughts were broken when Kelly came down the stairs, saying, "Found it!" She disappeared into the dining room for a moment then came back in. "Now where were we? Oh yes, Mandy. What have you decided about joining us for Christmas?"

"I'd love to come. Thanks for having me, Kelly."

"And that's fine with you?" She looked at Abby, locking onto her gaze.

Abby convinced herself Kelly's stare didn't look challenging. "Of course, I have some plans of my own for the holidays. We can work things out beautifully."

"Oh yes, the corporate lawyer boyfriend. Richard told me about him. How is he doing?"

"Very well, thank you," said Abby, but Kelly wasn't listening. Abby followed her gaze to the family photo she had examined earlier. Abby could swear the expression on Kelly's face was wistful.

Abby took advantage of the lull to say, "I think I should make a move for home now. It was a lovely dinner, Kelly. Thanks for inviting me."

Kelly looked happy once more. "It's early yet. Have another glass of wine."

"Thanks, but no." Kelly was usually a good actress but couldn't, or wouldn't, disguise the relief that flashed across her face. Abby stood. "How about you, Mandy? You're staying here for the night?"

"Yes, Mom. I'll give you a chance to have some time alone with Matthew. I have to head back day after tomorrow anyhow. I'm AWOL from classes, but I couldn't miss Matthew's birthday bash. I've only got a week or so until Christmas break so I'd better get back to some serious studying." She gave Abby a big hug and said, "I'll talk to you and maybe come over for coffee before I go."

"I'll see if Matthew and Richard have finished their man-to-man yet. I also need to find where I put my purse."

"I put it in the bedroom with your coat," said Kelly. "If you're sure you have to leave, I'll get them for you."

Abby gave Mandy another quick hug and headed for the dining room to see if the men had finished with reminiscing about fishing.

They were sharing a laugh as she walked in, and she marvelled at how alike they looked. Matthew had all his father's genes relating to appearance. They were both tall and lean—the type of lean that never had to worry about that extra piece of cake, thought Abby, still conscious of her straining waistband. Their hair was the same chestnut brown with a tendency to curl when it got too long, and they both had irresistible smiles and the ability to charm. She stood for a moment, admiring the picture until they put on their serious faces, and Richard closed the album.

"I imagine you're ready for home?" he said.

"I hate to drag you away from the journey down memory lane, but yes, I think it's getting late."

Matthew jumped up. "I'll run upstairs and grab my things. Be ready in a minute, Mom."

"Sorry if I monopolized Matthew this visit, but you still have two days to catch up."

Abby intended to make the most of them. "Why don't you come to the airport when I drop him off? We can both spend time with him while he waits for boarding call."

"I'll do that. Thanks, Abby." He seemed to recognize the reserve in her tone and added, "I'm sorry about not talking to you before inviting Mandy out at Christmas, but it just sort of popped into the conversation."

"I understand, totally," said Abby, and she thought she did. She couldn't figure out why Kelly wanted Mandy to share part of her romantic getaway at Christmas, but she was pretty sure she had orchestrated the conversation just as she pleased.

"I have some plans to finalize, but I'll be going away for Christmas too." said Abby, not wanting to leave a "poor me" impression with Richard.

"Neil?" asked Richard.

"Yes, he wants me to meet him in Turks and Caicos, along with some friends." Richard and Neil had never met, but Mandy managed to keep her parents informed of each other's lives. The strange thing was she had the ability to do it in a way that never censured or favored either parent. That was why Abby had wondered about the flashes of impishness in the comments she had made about the spa holiday. Mandy normally displayed a rare diplomatic talent in someone so young. Maybe she was missing her calling.

Kelly appeared beside Abby, holding her coat and purse. Matthew was right behind her with his case and jacket. "Give me the keys, Mom, and I'll start the car to let it warm up a little."

"It's okay. I treated myself to Command Start for this winter." She pressed the remote and saw the responding, blinking light through the window.

"Call me before you leave," Richard said as he and Matthew shared a back-slapping hug. Abby saw a mist in her ex-husband's eyes and felt a responding moisture in her own. They had so little time to spend with him, but Matthew had chosen his life's work, and they were both very proud of him.

Mandy and Matthew made the rest of the goodnights brief.

The cold wall that hit Abby in the short walk to the car gave her an excuse to wipe her watering eyes with a tissue. She didn't want to appear maudlin in front of Matthew. Tonight had been a celebration after all, not a wake. There was no snow on the ground, but the thermometer reading was close to record lows. She wished the snow would come. It usually brought warmer temperatures. She and Matthew slid onto the cold hard seats. The car would take a few minutes to warm up. When she had finally traded in her old beater on a new car last month, Abby had laughed at the idea of seat warmers. Now, she was glad of them and used them all the time.

"Fancy a quick tour first?" she said to Matthew. "The lights are all on along the river, and the view's better than ever this year. Maybe we can see some of the best house displays, too."

"Sure," said Matthew. "There used to be one street in the east end that was out of this world. Every house had a theme."

"Still is. Let's go there first."

By the time they got to the river, the car was toasty. They sat and enjoyed the view for a while with the motor running. Then Abby turned onto the side road that followed the river.

They oohed and aahed as they drove the access road along the lit up river's edge with huge colored light displays. There were cartoon scenes, an *Alice in Wonderland*, and of course, a Christmas pageant. Holiday music played through unseen speakers.

"Too bad we didn't have our skates," said Matthew, watching the well muffled skaters gliding along between light displays. "We used to come here at least once a year and skate the river."

Abby shivered. "Not tonight, thank you. It usually isn't this cold at the end of November, or am I just getting too old?"

Matthew grinned. "I'll never think of you or Dad as old. You both enjoy life too much. But you're right, it is cold. Maybe it will warm up tomorrow."

"Let's come back tomorrow night. We'll dress warmly, and I know your old skates are around somewhere."

"Deal. Now let's go home and get warm, and I'll beat you in a game of scrabble before bed."

"Peppermint cocoa and scrabble sounds wonderful. But we'll see who beats whom."

Matthew did, in fact, trounce her on the first game, but she nearly caught him on the second one, helped by a substantial word score on a double triple. Her score still wasn't high enough to win.

It was after midnight when they called it a night. Abby knew Matthew would be asleep instantly. He had a lot of practice falling asleep in unfamiliar places. Abby wasn't exactly an insomniac, but it usually took a chapter or two of reading to get her sleepy. She looked at her bedside clock and decided it was much too late to call Neil and say she had planned to accept his invitation. It was even an hour or two later where he was. He had e-mailed her the itinerary though, so she pulled her laptop across her knee and looked to see what seats were left for holiday travel. She was lucky enough to find one that fit closely with Neil's scheduled arrival and booked it. *There!* All done.

Now, of course, she was even less likely to get to sleep because she was looking forward to her trip. Maybe sleep would come if she pictured herself on a tropical beach with Neil. Nope. She didn't like the picture she had of herself with the excess pounds she'd added the last month or two. Funny, slim Neil never seemed to mind, so maybe she shouldn't either. After all, what were five extra pounds? Or ten, she corrected.

She rummaged through the books behind her in the bookcase headboard. Val McDermid? No, too intense and dark to induce sleep. Dickens? Too dreary and sad. Instead she picked up an old Josephine Tey mystery, *Daughter of Time*. She'd read it years ago. In the book, the hero policeman investigated a centuries old crime that she found fascinating.

Chapter Two

The two days left of Matthew's visit weren't long enough. Matthew told Abby wonderful stories about his work and the people he'd met. She talked to him about Neil. They reminisced a lot and went through some old photo albums.

Mandy came over the next day and took her brother to spend the afternoon with some old friends. Abby and Matthew waited one more night to go skating amongst the lights on the river. The weather turned a lot warmer. They laughed a great deal, and Abby cried a little when she finally had to put her son on the plane. Richard met them at the airport. Kelly wasn't with him this time. It interfered with her yoga class. Abby was thankful for yoga.

"Fancy a coffee?" Richard asked as the plane lifted from the runway,

"Sure."

They got their coffee in takeaway cups. Abby looked hungrily at the raspberry filled doughnuts on display but pushed the picture aside. She was already worried about fitting into her bathing suit. She wasn't about to make the situation worse.

They strolled over and took seats at a table by a window. "You sure you're okay with Mandy coming with us for Christmas?" asked Richard.

Abby was a little miffed, not about Mandy going, but

about the way everyone seemed to assume she would be upset, like she had no life of her own to live. She wasn't about to admit that maybe she didn't. Besides, she now had her own plans in the works. "Of course. I'll still get to spend time with her afterwards, before she has to go back to school. She'll love the trip. I'm a bit envious though. I love the island. That's where I went to college."

"It's where we met."

She looked quickly at him with a sideways glance. "Yes. It was. Christmas seems to bring out the nostalgia in us all."

"We had a lot of good years."

"And some not so good," countered Abby.

"My fault, mostly. I am sorry, Abby. I always had such good intentions to try harder to be a model husband."

"I didn't want model," she said tartly. "I just wanted faithful."

"I'm sorry," he said again.

"Water under the bridge."

Their conversations didn't usually take this side trip into the past. Usually their meetings, although friendly, were for sorting schedules or talking about the kids. That was when they talked at all. Even amicable, their divorce left a slight bitter taste.

Richard changed the subject. "You mentioned going to the Turks and Caicos Islands for the holidays? You'll be having a more exotic Christmas than we will."

"Oh, I don't know. Mine doesn't offer séances and crystals." She felt better after getting her dig in. "Yes, it's only for a week, but I could do with some warmth and sunshine. I never was a winter girl."

"You learned to skate and ski."

"And I never was much good at either. The kids must get their athletic skills from you."

"Did you ever picture the kids, when they were younger, turning out the way they did?'

Abby laughed. "Not really. For a couple of years I thought I might end up strangling Mandy." She looked at him accusingly. "She never rebelled against you. It was always me she threw tantrums at."

"It's all a gender thing, I guess. Matthew wasn't the rebellious type, but we still had a few confrontations, and I bet he never raised his voice to you."

"Hmm. Maybe." She had a sudden thought. "This trip you and Kelly are going on, it's not for a special reason is it?"

"What do you mean? It's for Christmas. That's special."

"Oh, I thought maybe the reason you wanted Mandy there was to turn it into an engagement bash or a wedding caper."

"*Caper?* You do have a way with words. No, if we ever decide to get married, we'll do it planned and proper with Matthew and the rest of the family there as well."

Abby thought for a moment he was going to include her in the guest list, but he stopped short of that. "What about Kelly's family? Does she ever talk about them?"

"She had a few issues with them growing up. Her mother is dead, and she doesn't have any contact with her father. She doesn't talk about them much."

Abby felt another pang of sympathy for Kelly. That must have been why she looked so longingly at the family picture on Richard's wall. "That's sad. Does she have siblings?"

"No. She was adopted and an only child. Funny thing is, she never knew about the adoption till she was grown up. Her adoptive mother told her on her death bed."

"How odd. Usually, kids get told about their adoption circumstances. The information could be important if there were genetic health issues. But everyone isn't the same. Good thing, I guess. Keeps us from getting bored with each other."

"I was never bored with you, Abby." Richard leaned over and touched her hand.

Abby moved away. "Let's not go there. I better get back and make my getaway plans. Ajax isn't going to like being left with a minder."

"You still have that cat? He must be getting on now."

"He is, but so am I." She knew Richard was about to make some gallant speech about her not aging, but she could do without his platitudes and quickly said, "Don't say it." She stood up. "I'm off then. I do hope you and Kelly have a great Christmas."

"You too."

She felt his eyes on her back as she left. Richard could usually tell what she was thinking, but she had never quite plumbed the depths of his mind, even after all these years. In spite of his seemingly open, outgoing and rather charismatic personality, he kept a part of himself unrevealed, even to his wife of over twenty years.

Back at home, Abby tackled her wardrobe problems. She could do with a quick shopping excursion, she thought, but there weren't too many shops that carried summer stock in December. So she'd have to make do. She tried on all her last year's shorts and tops as well as a couple of dressier outfits. They fit a little more snugly than they did a year ago, but as she turned in the mirror, it didn't seem to show. If she could keep on the straight and narrow diet-wise till she left, these should work okay.

Neil called her the moment he heard she was able to join him on the trip to Turks and Caicos. He offered to pick her up at the airport. He was going to get there a day before she did. The sound of his voice distracted her from Matthew's absence and thoughts of missing her family during Christmas.

Abby arranged for her next door neighbor to look after Ajax and check her plants and mail while she was gone. She felt a little lost for the next week and a half, waiting for her holiday, unable to concentrate on work where she freelanced in the field of education, writing instruction programs and textbooks. She was between projects at the moment, so nothing was pressing. The rest of the world was buying turkeys, making pumpkin pies and mincemeat tarts, and baking shortbread, but, this year, she could pass on all that.

She put her tree up and decorated it, the old tree she and Richard had used for years. It stood in the corner of the living room just to the side of the big window. This would be the third Christmas since their divorce. She had kept the house when they had split. Mandy had still lived at home then, so Abby had tried to keep everything the same as it always had been—the same furniture, the same traditions, the same habits. Now, maybe it was time for a change. When the holidays were over, she would redecorate. She gave a little shudder at the thought of parting with a big slice of her life, but they were just furnishings, just objects. The memories, she would keep.

Not knowing Mandy's plans or timing, she trimmed the tree on her own. When the kids were little, it had always been Mandy's job to put the angel on the top, lifted by her brother. Abby had always liked having the tree up early. She loved the Christmas feeling and wanted it to start as soon as possible. On the other hand, she always took the decorations down as soon as Christmas was over. When it was done, it was done. She resolved to do something similar with her life now. Richard was gone, she had her own relationship, and it was time to move out of the past. Maybe she would hire a decorator instead of relying on her own ideas. Heaven knew her style was haphazard at best. Left to her own devices, she'd probably end up with different furniture, but the same style, and that's not what she wanted, not what she needed.

She spent some time catching up on her correspondence. There weren't too many Christmas cards this year. Not the number she used to get when she and Richard were married. It seemed they had split their friends just like they had split their assets, and their divorce had been amicable by most standards. A lot of people didn't bother with cards. They sent long e-mail greetings or e-cards nowadays. Abby hated those. They had no personality. On the other hand, she still got her yearly cards packed with long letters from her old college friends, and she loved them. She'd long ago sent hers out.

It was two days before her scheduled flight when she got the call from Mandy.

"Mom?" Her voice was shaky and uncharacteristically soft.

Icy tentacles crept down Abby's spine, her "mother's intuition" sending off warning alarms. "What is it, Mandy? What's wrong?"

"Kelly's dead, Mom. The police were here, and they think someone killed her. They have Dad at the station asking him questions. You have to come."

Chapter Three

"Kelly's dead? Dead how?"

"They found her downstairs in the whirlpool bath. She took a big bash on her head. The police think someone did it."

"Why are they questioning your father? Why would they think he had anything to do with it?"

"I don't know, Mom, but I think someone said they heard them having an argument. I can't talk about it on the phone. I don't know what to do. Please, come."

"Of course. I'll grab a flight as soon as I can."

She never considered declining for a moment. She didn't owe Richard any favors, but she couldn't reject an appeal for help from her daughter. Mandy sounded terrified. What if they arrested her father?

Kelly dead? It was difficult to imagine. She'd rarely met anyone so energetic and full of life. And murdered? It was preposterous to think of Richard hurting anyone, let alone a woman he loved. Maybe Mandy was overreacting. Maybe the police were just talking to Richard because of their relationship. Maybe the head injury came from falling in the tub. Maybe...but it was useless to speculate.

She checked her options for a flight. It wasn't easy. Finally, she found a vacant seat on a site she had tried earlier without success. Someone's Christmas plans had taken a nosedive. She booked it quickly before it was snapped up. No seat sales here. At holiday time, it was full price everywhere.

She texted Mandy with her arrival time and slipped out to ask her neighbor Josie to look after Ajax a little earlier than planned.

How was she going to tell Neil? She decided an e-mail was the coward's way out and called him. She got hold of him on his cell and briefly described the problem. Surprisingly, he didn't sound at all put out by her change of plans.

"Of course, you have to help Mandy. She must be upset, not knowing what's going on. Just let me know how things work out. Maybe we can get away sometime after the holidays."

Part of Abby wished he'd been a little more disgruntled, but she knew it was just her usual lack of self-confidence where men were concerned niggling away at her.

She had a sleepless night. She put her cell on the bedside table and charged it. If there were any new developments Mandy might try to call her even if it were night time. Ajax sensed something was amiss and added to her insomnia. He kept waking her by butting his nose against her head, looking for attention or reassurance.

The snow started again the next morning, and the winds picked up. She worried all the way to the airport that flights might be cancelled. It put her normal flying fears into high gear, worrying about all the added dangers bad weather added to a flight.

Nothing was cancelled, but her flight was delayed by an hour, so she had lots of time at the airport to fret and fume. She hadn't had time to refill her prescription for Ativan, so she ordered a double rum and coke to settle her flying nerves. She looked around guiltily as she gulped the drink, but no one was paying attention to the wild lady drinking double shots so early in the day.

She surprised herself by dozing on the plane. She'd never done that before. It may have been the reassurance of the drink, or it may have been that she was too tired from last night's lost sleep. In any event, the flight seemed short and when she woke, they were ready for a landing at Vancouver. Landings she could handle. It was the take-offs that held her stiff with fear. She had a short transfer to make in Vancouver to a flight across to Comox. There was no time for the reassurance of another drink before she had to board. She gritted her teeth and clenched the armrests.

Mandy was waving to her as she came through the arrivals area. She ran into Abby's arms the way she did as a child, sobbing into her mother's embrace.

It only took a minute for her to compose herself and turn back into the adult she had become. "I'm so glad you're here. Maybe you can help sort them out."

"Sort who out?"

"The police. They think Dad killed Kelly."

"Have they arrested him?"

"No, but they've talked to him twice, and I think he's scared. He just tries to hide it from me."

Abby stopped short. "I just had a terrible thought. I booked the flight, but I never stopped to see if they had a room at the spa. They might not have one available."

"That's fine. You can bunk with me. I'd like that, and my room has two beds."

Abby watched the luggage coming by and spotted her one case with the purple cow tag that identified it apart from all the others. She grabbed it from the belt and said, "Okay, let's get out of here. You can tell me all about everything on the ride there."

By the time they got sorted from the traffic tangles of the airport and were on the highway heading to the spa, Mandy felt free to concentrate on her story.

"I don't really know a lot more than what I told you on the phone," she began slowly.

"Just start with when you arrived," said Abby, "and tell me in chronological order what happened, everything that happened, even the mundane things. That way, I'll get a better perspective."

The highway traffic was moderate. The driving was much smoother than Abby remembered on old Island Highway. The old highway meandered along the coast, passing through small communities on the way, offering picturesque views. The down side was the travel time. With slower speed limits, it took forever to travel the length of Vancouver Island. What made it worse was there wasn't much opportunity to pass on the two lanes. This highway was quick, but boring, and the speed limit was 120 km.

Abby turned her attention to her daughter's narrative.

"Okay, I'll start at the beginning. I arrived day before

yesterday, got settled and had an early dinner with Dad and Kelly. Everything seemed normal to me, except Kelly was more subdued than usual. She didn't rule the conversation the way she normally does. She seemed to be off in another world. Then Jessie, the receptionist, took me on a tour of the treatment rooms and showed me what was available. I decided to wait to see what Kelly had planned before booking anything. Instead, I went to the salon and got a manicure and my hair done. Are you sure you want to know all these things? They don't have anything to do with what happened."

Abby nodded. "You never know what might be significant later."

Mandy continued. "Dad asked me to come to their room after my hair appointment. That's when I noticed Kelly was really acting differently from her normal together self. She was pacing the room, not paying any attention to the conversation. She looked like she was waiting for something to happen."

"What did your dad say?"

"Nothing much. He looked like he was trying to pretend everything was normal. But it wasn't. I was beginning to wonder if it was me."

"You? Why?"

"Well, maybe Kelly had second thoughts about my interrupting their romantic getaway."

"She was the one that insisted you come."

"Only because Dad asked me first, and she wanted to make it look as though it had been her idea. I don't really think she wanted me along. It was just pretend."

"That's not the impression she gave me at Matthew's party," said Abby. She remembered Kelly's smirk when she'd asked Abby if it was all right with her for Mandy to come, and that's when it hit her that Kelly was actually dead. Up to that point, her mind had simply recorded Kelly's death as an event in Mandy's life. Now, she thought sadly of all that energy and beauty snuffed out so quickly and felt her eyes mist over. Richard was surely going through hell.

"So what next?" Abby prompted.

"Nothing. I said goodnight. I told them I'd see them at breakfast, and I went to my room. I was tired. I woke up in the morning to Dad pounding on my door."

"He found Kelly?"

"No. At that point, he just knew she was missing. He'd hoped to find her with me. Apparently, she and Dad had a fight the night before and she left. When she didn't come back, he thought she was mad at him. He assumed she got her own room or came to stay with me. When he realized that wasn't the case, that's when he got worried."

"And then?" Mandy's foot got heavy on the accelerator, and Abby kept one eye on the speedometer. She didn't want to comment, but they were virtually flying down the highway in the fast lane. She strained to hear any signs of sirens. If she went any faster, Abby would have to call her on it.

But Mandy apparently got a glimpse of Abby's stiff posture, and her gaze locked on the speedometer as she slowed. "Sorry, I was going too fast. I just want to get back and get things sorted. It's too awful to understand."

"It's all right. You know how nervous I am in fast cars. You weren't driving dangerously or anything, just faster than I'm used to. But go on. What did you and Dad do then?"

"We went to reception. Dad asked Jessie if she had seen her or if she had taken another room. Jessie said no, so we asked her to look around to see if she was in any of the treatment rooms. Nothing was open yet, but Jessie said she'd look. A while later, it seemed like forever, she came running up the stairs and said, 'We have to call an ambulance.' The manager came out, or maybe she came out earlier. I can't remember. She said to be sure the police came, too, and then it just became chaos. Dad wanted to go to Kelly, but Mona— that's the owner—wouldn't let him. She said everyone had to stay put till the police got there. She took us into the office to wait. I kept wondering what had happened. Dad paced the floor the whole time, and he didn't say a word."

"Did you know she was dead then?"

"No. Jessie had only said to call the ambulance. She didn't say she was dead. That's why Dad wanted to go to her. He thought she was lying somewhere sick or hurt, and no one was helping. He kept saying he had to go see her, and Mona called Theo, the masseur, to stand guard at the office door so he couldn't leave."

"What made the police think it wasn't an accident? Was her head under the water? Did it look as though she struggled with someone?"

"Jessie said she was just lying there in the whirlpool. She

had slumped over, and her head was under water. But there was blood, too. We thought she had fallen and hit her head. We assumed she was knocked unconscious and drowned."

"That sounds the most likely scenario. If she was upset with your dad, maybe she thought the whirlpool would relax her. Kelly doesn't think too much of rules, so it wouldn't bother her it was after hours. Were the doors unlocked?"

"The door to that area is kept locked, but any guest key will open it. The anteroom is also kept locked. It takes a manager's key to open that. There's a chain barricade across the stairs to the hydra section with a closed sign. I suppose anyone could just slip in. But the lights were dimmed, and none of the jets or anything in the different sections could be turned on without a staff key, so what would be the point of sneaking in?"

Mandy took a deep breath and went on, "The police wouldn't tell us much. Jessie is the one that told us how she found her. Her clothes were thrown into a pile beside the whirlpool, and that doesn't sound like Kelly. She was always so careful with her outfits. And neat. Almost obsessively neat."

"Maybe if she was upset..." Abby discarded the thought as soon as she said it. From what she'd seen, obsessive people became even more so when upset, as a means of getting back control.

"Oh darn! I missed our exit. I should have turned there." Mandy kept her eyes swivelled back on the missed exit after they'd passed for so long Abby watched the road ahead for her. It was a technique she'd perfected over the years while travelling in the passenger seat, ineffective, but it beat screaming. She wished she'd insisted on driving. Do all parents think their grown children drive like they're still a ten-year-old controlling a toy bus?

"We'll just take the next one and double back."

Abby unclenched her teeth and her hands, as Mandy's gaze was now directed in front of her again.

"Not so easy on this road. It could be a long time. Oh no, we're okay. There's a turnoff already. We can circle around and head back. Sorry, Mom."

"I should have let you concentrate on the road. Let's just get to the spa. You can tell me the rest when we get there." Abby tried to relax and assure herself Mandy was probably a better driver with quicker reflexes than her mother.

They turned off the main highway at the next exit, the right one this time, and followed a smaller highway that ran parallel for a while. Then they turned off down a secluded, well treed road. The sign at the turnoff was massive. The name, Ultimate Island Spa, was emblazoned across the top. Beneath it, a series of outlined pictures showed a well-endowed middle-aged woman in a mud bath, a blonde beauty getting a massage from an Adonis, and a family in swimwear in a rainforest of water. There was still room below for a quite readable phone number to call for reservations.

There was only a skiff of snow left along the road verge. Winter didn't hit the island with the severity she was used to on the prairies. She remembered the mild winters when she used to live here. Some winters, there was no snow at all. Others had a huge dump fall, but even then, it usually didn't last long. Today, the trees loomed large and green on both sides. Abby knew the ocean was nearby but saw no glimpse of it through the forest. A turn sign directed them to the left, over a bridge that spanned a creek, and suddenly they were in the open.

The main building was huge and white. It looked as though it had been built in stages and the result was a lack of symmetry. To the left was the three-storied, main block with a columned entrance at midpoint. It must have been the original hotel. The attachment to the right was T-shaped and much more functional-looking. It appeared to have more than one entrance. The one at the front appeared to lead into a dining room. A wide pathway led around the side. A second floor had a balcony extending along the front and around the corner. This wing, too, had a third floor. Three smaller buildings, painted the same dazzling white, formed a triangle beyond the addition, becoming visible as they followed the parking sign around the hotel side to a lot in the rear.

Mandy parked in a slot marked for guests and pulled Abby's case from the trunk. "We can go in the back way. The room key lets us in."

Abby took a deep breath and followed her daughter. It looked like the spirit of Christmas was going to be a little delayed this year. How could you celebrate a holiday with joy when someone you knew had just died violently?

Chapter Four

Abby followed Mandy down a corridor that ran to the front of the building. The reception desk was just in front of the main doors.

In honor of the season, a large silver Christmas tree decorated in gold stood in the corner by a marble fireplace. Garlands hung above both front doors as well as over the mantle. A rather bland medley of Christmas music came through unseen speakers.

A young girl sitting behind the desk stood quickly with a smile as they approached. She had dark brown, curly hair which was trapped behind her ears by a pair of barrettes. She wore black pants with a shimmery gold and silver top that echoed the lobby Christmas tree. On her left shoulder, a huge Santa and Rudolph pin twinkled gaudily at them. A name tag on the other side stated Jessie. She, or someone, had draped a garland around the desk chair. This was the girl that had been sent to look for Kelly and had found her in the whirlpool.

"Hello, Miss Addison. This must be your mother?"

"Yes," replied Abby quickly, wanting to get the formalities over as soon as possible. She'd come back to talk to Jessie later.

"Will you be staying with your daughter or do you require your own room? We have rooms available if you like."

"No thanks. I'll stay with Mandy. It will be simplest."

"I'll get you another key." She reached into a drawer and pulled out a card, swiping it through a programmer before handing it to Abby in a little pouch on which she wrote 214 in large neat numbers.

"I'm so sorry about... I mean, I'm sorry for your loss." Jessie seemed a little uncertain about how to express condolences to the ex-wife of the fiancé of the dead woman.

Abby understood and just said, "Thanks." She was uncertain too.

A middle-aged woman with streaked hair in several shades of blonde approached from the elevator. She wore a long, brocaded robe, and her hair looked slightly damp. "Jessie, I need some more coffee in my room. I can't find anyone in housekeeping."

"I'm sorry, Gran. I'll bring some up in a moment."

"No need. Mona has some in the office. I'll grab a pouch from there."

She walked past Jessie into the office, and Abby wondered if she could be one of the owners. *Gran?* Maybe the place was a family-run venture. She assumed Mona was the manager. She read the words on the door after it closed again, and her guess was confirmed. Mona Davenport, Operator. That possibly meant manager, owner or both.

They opted for the elevator even though their room was just one flight up. Once in the room, Mandy put Abby's case on the bed closest to the door. "Sorry. I took the window one. We can trade if you like."

"Of course not. This is fine. Besides, I'm closer to the bathroom here." She plopped her suitcase open and began to unpack.

"Top two drawers are empty," said Mandy, pointing to the large dresser.

Abby quickly filled them and took a load of toiletries to the bathroom.

Mandy put a coffee pouch into the hotel coffee maker and poured water through. "I need something to perk me up," she said. "It's been a long day already and there's still a lot to go."

Abby would have preferred a glass of wine, but the coffee was likely a wiser choice.

"I'm just going to let Dad know we're back." Mandy dialed his room. Abby wandered to the window and looked out. It was a peaceful scene—woodsy and clean. The trees were green for the most part. The little bit of snow that had fallen hadn't penetrated the woods. The vista in front of her could belong to any season. This wasn't the type of place you expected death, definitely not a murder. The spa owners were surely concerned. A murder on their property was not good advertisement.

She turned back as Mandy set the phone down. "Dad wants us to go over there as soon as you're settled. He wants to talk to you. He can tell you a lot more about what happened and what the police said."

Abby would have preferred to hear it from her daughter, but knew she was right.

"Okay, let me take a quick shower first. You know how I am with flying, and I need a de-stressor before we talk to your dad."

Abby turned the water as hot as she could stand it while she washed and shampooed. Then she slowly switched it to lukewarm. The warm spray took away the tight band across her forehead, and she began to relax. By the time she towelled off and pulled on a clean pair of gray slacks and a white blouse, she felt nearly human again.

She was still rubbing her hair with the fluffy white spa towel when she came into the room. She was startled to see Richard sitting on the edge of one of the beds. He was leaned over with his hands clasped together. He lifted his head with a grim smile.

"Sorry," he said, "but I didn't want to stay in that room any longer. I thought we could talk here just as easily."

Abby put her hand up to hide her face in an automatic gesture. She felt as though she'd been caught flat-footed, standing there with no makeup and damp, twisted hair. Then she thought of the reason for their meeting, and it didn't seem to matter.

She crossed the room to Richard. He stood, and she hugged him as though he were her child rather than her ex-husband.

"How are you holding up? Oh, that's a silly question. By the last one of your nerves, I imagine."

"Thanks, Abby. I haven't had time to wrap my mind around the idea that Kelly's gone. The police have rather kept me occupied. I don't even know if I can arrange a funeral for her or when. They ask a lot of questions, but they sure don't answer any."

"They didn't say they seriously think you killed Kelly?"

Richard winced a little at the word "killed," and said, "I honestly don't know. They tell me they're considering her death suspicious and ask a lot of questions about our relationship."

"You did have an argument with her?"

Richard sighed and sat down on the edge of the bed again. "It was this whole trip," he said. "I didn't want to come here. Kelly arranged it from start to finish out of the blue, and I wanted to know why."

"That's what the argument was about?" It didn't sound like a topic serious enough to end in an extreme confrontation.

"Sort of."

"Okay, start at the beginning. It was Kelly's idea to arrange a getaway?"

Richard assumed his original posture, not looking at either Abby or Mandy, twisting his hands around each other as he spoke. "The original idea to take a trip was mine. It didn't start out as a big deal. We were going to spend a week in a posh hotel in Victoria. Then Kelly decided she wanted to go to a spa. Not just any spa, it had to be this one."

"Why this one?"

"She gave me a long speech about discovering spiritualism and other nonsense about pyramid power and crystals. She said she was interested in it, and that's why we had to come here. I went along with it. Kelly gets these ideas sometimes, but they usually fizzle out." Abby and Mandy exchanged looks of agreement. "Then, that night, I discovered her real reason for choosing this spa."

"Which was?"

"Look, I don't know how much you know about Kelly."

"Not much."

"I think I told you at the airport that she was adopted? That she didn't get on with her father?"

"You said she didn't know she was adopted until her mother died."

"Oh good. I did tell you about it. Anyhow, she tried to track down her birth mother earlier with no luck. There was a no contact clause in the adoption contract. Then, out of the blue, her birth mother phoned last month. She was out here on the coast and wanted to meet."

"So she told you all this?"

"No, not at first. That's why I was upset. She didn't know if she wanted to renew contact or not, so she didn't say anything. She just gave me a big song and dance about her new interests, and that's why we had to come to this spa."

"So why did the meeting have to be here instead of Victoria?"

"Today, I found out her mother has a share in this spa, and some of her family is here, too. Her mother had the same idea as Kelly—to meet and see how it went before breaking it to the family. If everything went well, Kelly could meet the family, and if things didn't go right, they could just back away. She didn't even give Kelly her real name."

"Sounds a little bit like mother like daughter," piped up Mandy.

"Did she meet her mother?" Abby went on.

"I don't know. She had a meeting arranged that night. I asked her where she was going. She wouldn't say, so I said I was going with her, and then finally she told me that her mother was here. I was angry she hadn't told me earlier. We had words. Unfortunately, we were overheard when we took the argument out of the room." Richard leaned forward and put his face in his hands. "It was a stupid argument, and we would have made up in the morning. I can't even remember what we said." Finally, he sat up and said, "And that's the last I saw of her. When she didn't come back, I thought she was just getting back at me or sulking. I didn't get worried until morning. Of course, the police read a lot into that, too."

"Did she tell you her mother's name? Did you tell the police all about this? If they think someone killed Kelly in an emotional outburst, why wouldn't they be questioning the mother?"

"I told them, but I had the name wrong. I used the name she gave Kelly, which was Sylvia Daniels, and at first I'm sure they thought I was making it all up."

"But?"

"This morning they said they'd checked it out. They talked to the manager and there was no one here under the name she gave Kelly. It didn't take long for the police to figure out she was the manager's mother, Sylvia Davenport.

She planned the meeting here to see Kelly, and the manager had no idea about Kelly or the meeting."

"Well, that should let you off the hook! Or, at least give them somewhere else to cast their nets. She sounds like an odd woman to me. One minute she doesn't want to meet her long, lost daughter, the next she does. Maybe she changed her mind again. Maybe they had a fight about whether to tell the others. Or, maybe they did tell the others, and one of the family was angry with her."

"But she told the police she never saw Kelly. She said she waited for her, and she never showed."

"And they believe that?"

"Apparently a mother, even a long, lost one, has more credibility than an argumentative fiancé."

Abby knew Richard wasn't used to not being believed. He had certainly lied flawlessly to her before and managed to convince her everything was fine in their marriage when it wasn't. She shut off that line of thought. It had nothing to do with the present situation. She was sure everything Richard was telling them now was the truth. It was merely a matter of convincing the police.

Then the word fiancé hit her like a slap. So maybe Richard and Kelly were going to do a wedding on the quiet after all. Would that help or hinder his case with the police?

"So did you meet the mother?"

"No. I haven't seen her yet, but apparently the name Davenport is the name of the family that owns the hotel."

Abby and Mandy exchanged looks. "It must be the woman who went into the office and Jessie called Gran."

Mandy nodded. "She did look quite at home. She went into the office to get coffee. Your ordinary guest would never dare to just walk in to a private office."

"So, if she's the owner, that means Jessie is part of the family." Abby stopped to go over the check-in conversation in her mind. "The name on the door of the office was Mona Davenport, and you said Kelly's mother was Sylvia." She looked at Richard for confirmation. He nodded.

"If that's the case," said Mandy, "the whole family must be here. Mona might be a daughter? If Jessie called her Gran, does that make Mona her mother?"

"We'll have to find out." Abby paused. "We have to talk to Jessie."

"Whoa," said Richard. "What difference does it make if the whole family is here? Does it matter? Why would they have a reason to want Kelly dead? Wouldn't they be happy to have a new sister?" His words were met with two pitying glances. Men knew nothing of the nuances of sisterhood.

"Well, is Sylvia Davenport rich? Probably," Abby answered her own question. "Because if she owns or is part owner of this place, she must have a few bucks. Maybe the rest of her family decided Kelly was a threat to their inheritance."

Richard threw water on that idea. "If Kelly and her mother never met, then the rest of the family wouldn't know. The plan was to have the family in the background until they saw how the meeting went."

"That's maybe what Sylvia told the police, or maybe even what Kelly thought. That doesn't make it so. She could have been protecting them."

"We don't even know all their relationships yet," said Richard. "You're building up a whole story with very little to go on."

"Then we find something to go on," said Mandy. "Come on, Mom, let's go talk to Jessie and find out the whole family thing. She seems talkative enough, and it's pretty hard to say to a guest 'I won't tell you' to a friendly question."

Abby didn't rush to follow her daughter. Instead, she turned to Richard. "Why are the police so concerned about you and Kelly? A snatch of an argument and a relationship don't seem enough to get their spidey-senses in an uproar."

"Oh, I forgot to tell you about the lighter."

Mandy stopped with her hand on the door. "What lighter?" said Mandy and Abby together.

"My gold lighter. I've had it for ages."

"I thought you quit smoking," accused Abby with a frown.

"I started again." Richard ran his fingers through his hair where it curled over his forehead in a distracted gesture.

"So what about the lighter?"

"The police, well Jessie actually, found the lighter by the whirlpool where Kelly..." His voice trailed off.

"How did it get there?"

"I don't know."

"Are you sure it's yours?"

"Yes. It had my initials on it, remember?"

Abby pictured the lighter in her mind. It would be unmistakeable. As well as his initials, it had an etching of a fish of some sort, a pickerel she thought, not that it mattered.

"When did you last use your lighter?"

"Just before supper. Then, when I went to have a cigarette later that evening, I couldn't find it. Maybe I left it on the dinner table."

"Did you check with reception? Maybe someone turned it in?"

"No, I thought I'd just mislaid it. I was shocked when they found it with Kelly." Richard's voice had an uncharacteristic, hard edge to it.

"Sorry, Dad," said Mandy. She walked over to the bed and sat down beside him, her arm over his shoulders. "We're just trying to help. It's important to know when the lighter went missing so we can figure out how it got there."

"That's the police's job, surely." But he looked up at Mandy and patted her hand.

"Not if they think you had something to do with it. They might just pick who they think the most likely suspect is and look for evidence to support it. They won't be looking for anything to help you." As comforting speeches went, it wasn't exactly a winner, but Richard didn't seem to notice the words, only the love and support behind them.

"I guess not. Okay, go ask your questions and see what you can find out about Kelly's new family. I don't see how it will help, but I guess it's better than doing nothing."

"Speaking of help, have you talked to a lawyer yet?"

"No. I haven't been arrested or anything."

"Doesn't matter. Don't say anything else to the police or anyone until we find you a lawyer."

"Okay. I suppose you're right. I'll find someone." He picked up the phone book and thumbed through the yellow pages.

"Not like that!" said Abby. "Phone Mike."

"Mike's back home. He can't help from there."

"He'll still know lawyers all across the country and their reputations. He can recommend someone. Maybe he can even call someone for you and fast track representation."

Richard searched for his cell. "I have Mike's number on my phone. I left it in my room. I'll go call him."

"And remember, no talking to anyone till you talk to your lawyer first."

He left without looking back. This lost-sounding Richard was not the man Abby remembered being married to for over twenty years. He was usually decisive and in command. Now he acted more like a young boy waiting to be told what he should do. Abby didn't like it. She also didn't like where these thoughts led. If Richard was the small boy, she had taken the role of Mom. Was it the loss of Kelly or the shock of being questioned by the police that had shaken Richard to his roots? Probably a bit of both.

Now Abby was not only asking herself questions, but answering them as well. She looked at Mandy to be certain she hadn't spoken out loud.

"Let's go find Jessie," said Mandy.

Chapter Five

When they got to the lobby, Jessie was just coming back from taking a new guest on a tour. They waited until she was alone. She slipped through to the other side of the desk, sitting in the office chair, facing them.

"Hi," she greeted briefly, smiling, but looking at them dubiously as though not sure what to say next. Sudden death did that to people. Expressing routine condolences didn't seem to cover the situation.

"Would you mind if we asked you a few questions?" asked Mandy

"Of course not. How can I help you?" She stood, shuffling papers as they spoke. There didn't seem to be any purpose to her shuffling. She was probably trying to cover her uncertainty, thought Abby.

Abby took over the lead. "I'm sorry. We couldn't help noticing earlier that you called that lady, Sylvia, Gran. Is she your grandmother?"

"Why do you want to know?" A little suspicion crept into Jessie's voice. But she stopped her paper play and gave them her full attention.

"We know Sylvia is the one Kelly came to meet. She's her birth mother."

Jessie chewed her bottom lip. "I guess it doesn't hurt to talk about it now that everyone knows. I wasn't supposed to let on who she was before. Gran told me she was meeting someone and didn't want them to know her real name. She didn't say who it was. I didn't know it was the dead woman."

"Is she actually your grandmother?"

"No. She's my great-aunt. My grandfather is her older brother."

"And Mona, the manager. Where does she fit in?"

"Mona is my aunt. Gran is her mother—hers and Aunt Belinda's."

"Belinda? We haven't heard of her. She's here, too?"

"Belinda lives here. She and Mona are part owners. Belinda does the readings."

"Readings?"

"You know, the séances and tarot cards and other things. She's really good. You should try her before you go. Once she told a woman...." The words dried up as if Jessie's mind came back to the reason for their talk. She was certainly less restrained talking about things unrelated to the death, but that seemed natural.

"Oh. Are they all owners here?"

"Mona and Belinda are. So is my grandfather." Her face clouded at his mention.

"Is he here, too?"

"No," she sighed. "But I'm sure he'll be coming." Then she clammed up. "I shouldn't be talking about family business to you. And I'm busy, so if you don't need anything?" She returned to her paper shuffling and gave a glance at the phone as though willing it to ring. She certainly wanted to end this conversation.

"Sorry Jessie, but thanks. It must have been a great shock to realize you had another aunt."

"I didn't know. We didn't know. Gran never told us."

"Not even when Kelly arrived?"

"No. And I don't want to talk about Gran anymore. I don't want you to bother her either. Gran is the most wonderful person I've ever known, and she's terribly upset over what happened, so stay away from her, okay?" With that, she turned and retreated into the office. The interview, if that's what it was, was definitely over.

Back in the room, Abby said, "So what have we learned? And is any of it a help?" She picked up the empty coffee pot, then decided against making a fresh one. Her nerves were already tingling.

"Not much of a help since Jessie confirms they didn't know anything about Kelly beforehand. The police will think that rules out any motive."

"The big question is why did Sylvia change her mind? About contacting Kelly, that is? There must have been something specific to cause it. What changed in her life in the last year?"

"There's one way to find out. Let's ask her." Mandy was always one to prefer the direct route.

"That might not be so easy if the family is rallying around," said Abby. "Can we just walk up to the door and knock? Do we even know what room she's in? Jessie isn't going to tell us. So where else can we find out about her? Staff? Someone that's worked here for ages?"

"The only one I've met is Stephanie, the manicurist, and she's my age. She said she just started work here last month, so I don't think she'll be a help. I think she has a thing for the massage therapist, and that's why she applied to work here in the first place."

"Let's stroll through the building and see who might be a help. I want to have a look around the facilities anyhow. Can you handle a visit to the whirlpool?"

Mandy gave a slight shudder and said, "Sure. At least I never saw her there. The police let the spa open it up again."

They wandered through the spa corridors, past the stairs and elevators on the opposite side of the building to where the dining room sat, poking their heads around the entry to the water treatment. The door opened up into an open space with walls filled with pictures and photos of relaxing ocean and forest scenes. Stairs just inside the entry led up to the gym. A softly-lit reception area with soft ocean sounds in the background held two women wrapped in white terry robes, sipping on tea. They barely looked up, engrossed in their tranquility. There were comfortable chairs and a selection of herbal teas to start the journey to relaxation. Soft pastels lined the walls in colors designed to lower the blood pressure. A counter was filled with products that would be used to calm and soothe. Steps led down a rock-lined pathway to the lower level. They took a few steps downward, and they could see the pathway curved through a variety of waterfalls, rainforests, the sauna, and the hot and cold water therapy baths.

They weren't dressed, or rather undressed, properly to enter the waterfall zone, so they were only able to peer around the corner. An attendant in blue scrubs climbed the steps from below with an armful of towels. She paused to ask if they needed a tour, or if she could help them in some way. The translation was easy to grasp. She didn't want them there on their own. They politely said they were just looking and would book appointments later. The attendant smiled and walked up the staircase, looking back to be sure they followed. They retreated up the steps to the hallway.

Another set of steps to the left descended to a mud bath and shower area. The treatment area appeared to follow a near circle back to the area they had seen. To their right, a door led to a solarium with lounging chairs, more soft music and a view of the ocean. Stacks of white terry robes and fluffy towels filled the shelves beside the entry.

They had passed the hair salon earlier. It was in a separate area by the gift shop just off the lobby. Down the corridor were doorways labelled with descriptive pictures showing their purposes. One showed a pyramid, another was a large crystal, and yet another seemed to signify treatment with heated stones. The pyramid and crystal ones must have related to Belinda, the other sister. Abby tried one door tentatively, but found it, not only closed, but locked. The other treatment rooms were markedly deserted as well. Was it now past regular hours, or was the Christmas season unusually quiet, or had a death at the spa put a dampener on business? She looked at her watch. Five thirty. Maybe regular appointments ended at five. Or, maybe they took a break for dinner. She'd check the posted hours on her way out.

As they passed the massage room, the door stood slightly open. A tall, well-built man with the looks of an Adonis was putting away a stack of towels. He turned when he became aware of their presence. His smile was charming, and combined with his good looks, made him the epitome of a Greek god. His hair was streaked with sunshine, his skin glowed, and his eyes flashed with sensual power.

"Are you looking for a massage?" he asked. "I don't think I have a booking for you, but I have the next slot open. I'm Theo by the way." He held out his hand and shook both of theirs, holding Mandy's longer than necessary.

"Not right now," said Abby, noticing her daughter's eyes

lingering over Theo's excellent physique as she made no move towards reclaiming her hand. Abby felt impervious to his charm. He wasn't her type, and he was much too young, but if he could wow Mandy in spite of the circumstances, he was a dangerous man. This would be the man who enticed the manicurist to switch jobs so she could be near him. Abby wondered if any of the attraction was mutual.

"I recognize you," he said to Mandy. "It was your friend who died. I'm sorry."

"My father's friend actually, but thanks. You were the one who kept Dad cooped up in the office when he wanted to go to Kelly." Her admiring look was replaced by one of accusation.

Theo didn't take it personally. He merely smiled wider and said, "It had to be done. It would have complicated things for the police if he went there. And Jessie said she was definitely dead already, so he couldn't have done anything for her."

"He didn't know that!" Mandy's eyes flashed in anger. "Someone could have at least let us know."

"Sorry, it wasn't my call. I'm just the hired help. Mona only said to keep him in the office till help arrived. I do what I'm told."

Only when you want to, thought Abby. *I bet you're very good at getting what you want, especially if women are involved.* Out loud, she said, "Well, thanks for your sympathy, but we'd better get going." Then she added, "How were both you and Jessie here? The treatment rooms weren't open yet. Do you usually get here that early?"

"There's a wing above the treatment area with staff apartments. Some of us live in town. Some of us live here. It makes it easy, and they're nice apartments. Jessie and I live here."

"Who else amongst the staff lives here?"

"Well Mona, of course, and her sister Belinda, George, the maintenance man, Jessie and I. I think that's it. There are only a few apartments, so you have to have some pull to get one."

Abby could imagine the pull Theo had to get short-listed for an apartment. They hadn't met Mona yet, but maybe she was the type to feel Theo's charisma. No mention of Stephanie, so apparently, she didn't have the same pull and had to drive in to work from town. Or, maybe she just didn't need an apartment or didn't want to live so close to her job. You'd certainly have problems calling in with a fake illness living where you worked, or trying to be unavailable for overtime.

"Wow," said Mandy when they were out of hearing. "I bet he doesn't get that physique without some serious weight training."

"Maybe he uses steroids." Abby wanted to throw cold water on her daughter's admiration. Theo was not any mother's wish for a playmate for her daughter.

"He'd be a lot bulkier and awkward if he were on steroids. Instead, he's just, well, perfect."

"Hmmph," was all Abby could manage in reply.

"Sorry, Mom. We're off the subject. I was just admiring him like you would a prize stallion or a beautiful flower, not as a person. He's not my type." Abby wasn't so sure. She planned to keep him as far away as possible from her daughter. She wanted to question him more, but she was going to do it on her own.

She checked the hours of operation on the entry to the treatment area, and the hours were listed as ten to five and seven to nine. Theo must have kept to his own schedule. The exercise room was on the floor above and open much longer hours. Apparently, a room key admitted guests to the area so they could sweat on the machines to their heart's content before breakfast or after everyone else was in bed.

"It's almost time for dinner. We should check with your dad and see if he found a lawyer. Then we'll go for something to eat."

Chapter Six

They climbed the extra flight and knocked on the door of room 323. Richard had just come out of the shower. His hair was damp and curling, and he had on one of the spa robes. "Come in," he said. "Mike is a fast worker. He got hold of a good lawyer, and I have an appointment."

"When? Do you want one of us to go along?"

"Oh, I don't have to go to her office. She's coming here. She wants to see the place firsthand so she can get an idea of what happened when she talks to the police."

"She?"

Richard flashed a grin, showing some of his old spunk. "Not becoming a sexist, are you, Abby? She's supposed to be one of the best trial lawyers around."

"Trial? Do you think it's going to go that far?" Mandy looked as though she was about to cry, all thoughts of the Adonis seemingly gone from her mind.

"Don't worry. It's just preparation. She said she wants to stop it before it gets that far. She said I'm not supposed to talk to anyone about what happened until she gets here, even you."

"Even us?"

"Yes. She said family can sometimes be more of a hindrance than a help, and the less you know, the better."

Abby decided she wasn't going to like this new lawyer

much. But it didn't matter as long as she was good at her job and kept Richard out of jail. "What time do you want to go for dinner?"

He took a quick glance at his watch. "A little early, isn't it? It's not even six yet. The lawyer said she's coming right out, so I should talk to her alone over dinner when she gets here. You two go along whenever you want."

Abby felt as though they were being dismissed for a more important woman. She was surprised at the impact with which that thought hit her. After all, she had dropped everything to rush out to help. *Don't be childish*, she told herself. *This is about things much more important than your injured feelings. Kelly is dead, and Richard is under suspicion. This lawyer is his best chance at absolution. Get over it!*

"Let's go for a look around the gift shop, Mom, and then we'll get dinner," Mandy looked a little put out at her father's dismissal, too.

"My stomach is still a couple of hours ahead of you," said Abby. "I guess that's why it's complaining."

They left the room and took the enclosed first flight of stairs and then the wide twisting staircase down to the lobby. "I'm glad this lawyer seems to be quick and on the ball," said Abby, trying to keep the doubt out of her voice. "But if she's so good, why is she able to clear her table so fast to take on a new client?"

"Probably because this has been in the news, and she's seeing it as a high profile case. That would get her points professionally."

Chapter Seven

Jessie was at her desk, opening envelopes with a shiny silver letter opener that looked sharp and dangerous. She seemed to like bling, Abby thought, judging from her jewelry, sequined top, and the elaborate Christmas emblems she sported. Abby wondered if she ever had days off, or if there were part-time staff to give her breaks. Two men approached the desk, one of them carrying a briefcase. Jessie dropped the letter she was opening and slid the ornate opener into a desk drawer, slamming it shut with her knee. The two newcomers didn't look like your run-of-the-mill guests. You wouldn't expect to see a pair of businessmen booking a spa together. They were much too young to be the grandfather Jessie said would be on his way. Police? She debated slipping closer to see if she could make out what they were saying, but Mandy pulled her by the arm in the direction of the gift shop. Abby allowed herself to be redirected. She wasn't going to be able to overhear anything anyway. The shorter of the two men had noticed her lingering presence and cast a quick glance her way.

"Did you meet the police when they talked to Dad?" she asked Mandy.

"Meet isn't exactly the right word. They didn't introduce themselves, only asked who I was and when I got here. They took my name and address and said they wanted a statement later. It was Dad they concentrated on. The shorter, stocky one is the one who questioned us."

"We should go talk to them."

"Not now, Mom. We should see what they're doing here first. Maybe they're realizing it's silly to suspect Dad, and they're questioning the family more. Besides, we shouldn't talk to them until we hear what Dad's lawyer says."

"But what if they leave?"

"Not likely. Look." Jessie was ushering them into the office, and both men took off their coats as if they planned to stay for a while.

"All right," said Abby. "We can keep an eye on the office from the gift shop. It has an all-glass front, so we can see when they decide to leave."

The first display counter inside the gift shop held crystals, pyramids and boxes of smooth colored stones. The next one held a rack of lighters. An odd choice for a health-oriented spa to have, Abby thought. They seemed to want to cover all bases where their guests' needs were concerned. Maybe they used them to light candles, but Abby thought matches were more romantic than a lighter. Smokers staying at the Spa had to go outside to smoke, of course. They probably had a special spot, like most commercial ventures did. Abby was glad she'd given up the habit years ago, but sad to see Richard had backslid. A sudden thought came to her, but she shoved it aside nearly as soon as it appeared. She examined the rack, but no lighter looked like the one Richard had lost. That didn't mean there hadn't been one though. But Richard had said he lost the lighter, and if someone wanted to implicate him, surely they wouldn't be able to get one engraved with his initials and the fish, even if they had found an identical one. She was clutching at straws. It had to be Richard's lighter they found. Someone must have placed it there.

A woman of mature years approached them with a ready smile. Her name tag read Tillie. She was gaunt rather than slim, and the lines around her eyes and mouth put her at retirement age, if not over. Her hair was a soft, perfectly even silver that probably came from chemistry rather than natural aging. She wore a dark blue dress with no apparent waistline, likely designed to disguise her thinness. Strands of colored glass and wooden beads hung in two ropes around her neck, dangling to where her waistline would be.

"We're just having a quick browse before dinner," said Abby, trying to station her position so she could keep the office in view. "Are you ready to close? We don't want to keep you."

"We close in about fifteen minutes, but take your time. Let me know if you need any help." She looked as though she were going to walk back to the checkout counter when she turned and gave Mandy a close look. "Oh, you're the girl who was friends with the one who was killed. I am sorry."

"I'm Mandy," she answered. "It was my father's friend who died."

"So sad when something like that happens to someone so young. It's the first time anything like that has ever happened at the spa." The implication was that it was the victim's fault that anything as distasteful as death had sullied the premises.

Abby pushed aside the resentment she felt on behalf of Kelly and asked, "Have you worked here for a long time?"

"Ever since it opened ten years ago. Mona and Belinda did such a great job renovating the hotel and making all the additions." She waved a ring-covered hand around. "I knew the family from before, you know." Abby didn't know exactly what she meant, but accepted it as a figure of speech.

Since Tillie looked inclined to talk, she decided to prod her a little. "Mona and Belinda are sisters?"

"Yes. Mona is the one with the business sense. Belinda was always a little flaky, but she's a lot smarter than people give her credit for."

Abby realized they'd hit the mother lode of information about the family. Tillie had no qualms about talking to perfect strangers about her employers. Abby planned to make use of it.

"And their mother is here too, I think?"

"Yes." Tillie grinned. "Sylvia."

"Is she an owner too?"

"Not really. I think her husband put up the cash to start it, or at least secured it for the girls. He was the one with the bucks in the family."

"Was?"

"Yes, he died a few months ago. Had an accident. A rather horrible one." Tillie stopped for a moment. Abby didn't know if it was to take a breath, or if she was debating further comment on the accident. Whatever the reason, she said nothing more on the subject. "Now Sylvia has all the money, and she doesn't have to go hat-in-hand to the old geezer every time she wants her hair done. It's a lot easier on Belinda too." Abby noticed she didn't include Mona. Maybe she got along better with the old man than her mother and sister did.

"He was a bit of a tartar, was he?"

"Oh, the stories I could tell, but I'd better not." There was a limit to her indiscretion, apparently.

"So Mona and Belinda are the sole owners of the spa?"

"Oh no, Sylvia's brother, Arthur, has a share and so do two of his friends. Arthur and Edward were great pals."

"Edward? Was that Sylvia's husband?"

"Yes. Sylvia's brother, Arthur, is a real control freak, if I ever saw one. He and Edward were more like brothers than brothers-in-law. Between them, they kept poor Sylvia tied up in knots. You should see Jessie nearly reduced to tears every time Arthur comes for one of his visits. Not very grandfather-ly, huh?" Tillie broke into another smile. "I'll bet he'll be here soon. He won't want to think someone dared to die at the spa without asking his permission first."

Was Tillie this forthcoming with information to everyone, or was it just because they were involved in the drama that was happening around her? Maybe she expected that they would be just as talkative to her. Sort of tit for tat. Or, maybe bereavement meant that all normal rules went out the window.

Abby was keeping one eye on the office but couldn't see any movement past the closed door. She was sure the police hadn't left though.

"Arthur and his two monkey cohorts." Tillie was enjoying herself. Abby wondered what Mona would think about Tillie's information highway. Did she know how loose-tongued her employee was?

"Monkey cohorts?"

"Yes, you know the three monkeys—hear no evil, see no evil, speak no evil. That's what we call them. Well, it was Belinda who named them. She has a terrific sense of humor." Tillie gave a little giggle.

"Which one is Arthur?" Abby was frantically trying to sort out the family connections. "Arthur is Sylvia's brother, right? And he's Jessie's grandfather?"

"Yes, he's hear no evil. He simply won't allow it. Then, his old friend Jack—they went to school together—is see no evil. He doesn't believe in evil, so of course, he doesn't see it. He thinks the best of everyone."

"They sound like an unusual combination to be friends," prompted Abby.

"Oh, they are. Belinda says they met their first year at school and have been friends ever since. Jack needs someone to keep him from being taken by any conman who comes along, and Arthur likes being the lord protector, so it works out well for both of them."

It sounded as though Belinda and Tillie spent time together. Maybe Tillie would give them an "in" to talk to Belinda.

"Who's the third man? Another friend of Arthur's?"

"Oh no," said Tillie. "Arthur can't stand him. It was Mona who got him to invest. Arthur didn't meet him until it was too late. He's speak no evil. Actually, Moses doesn't speak much at all. Walks around with his mouth shut at all times."

Tillie appeared to realize she had exceeded the normal bounds of revelation to strangers and quickly changed to a professional conversation. "Well, if you see anything you like or have any questions, be free to ask." With that, she returned to her counter.

Mandy took Abby's elbow and pointed to the lobby. A woman in a dark skirt with a white blouse and a jacket draped loosely over her shoulders was on her way to the reception desk, walking with a purposeful step. She stopped behind the desk and from Jessie's attitude of deference, Abby guessed she was Mona. That was likely Tillie's reason to shut up. She didn't want Mona to know she was gossiping with the guests and suddenly realized how far she'd stepped out of bounds.

Tillie began the motions of closing shop, so they felt compelled to leave. The two policemen were outside the door of the office now, talking to Mona. Abby and Mandy hesitated at the foot of the stairs. They could hardly go barging over to interrupt the conversation, but they didn't really have an excuse to hang around.

Abby looked at the hair salon on the opposite side of the room. A closed sign hung on the door, but Abby saw two women moving around inside, doing cleanup. One was tall, slim, and at least middle-aged. The other was young with long blonde hair. Stephanie, the manicurist? It didn't matter much. They wouldn't be able to talk to her today. Abby was much more interested in what the men at the desk were doing.

The police probably wouldn't tell them anything. And they didn't have any new information to impart. Abby just wanted to be sure they were following up on Kelly's family connections as well as Richard. Maybe they would give up on him. Then she thought about the lighter. Until that was explained, she felt sure they wouldn't give up on Richard as a suspect.

The shorter of the policemen began to make a move, rising from his chair and setting it to the side. Mona gestured in the direction of the dining room. He picked up his coat and briefcase, and the two men walked in the direction Mona steered them.

"They're going to have dinner here," said Abby. "Let's try to get a seat close to them. Maybe we can hear what they're saying."

Mandy threw cold water on that. "I don't think two policemen are going to be shouting things in public that are confidential. Oh, I just remembered the name of the short one. He's Sergeant Woolly."

"I hope he's not," said Abby.

"Not what?" Mandy gave her a strange look.

"Woolly."

Mandy gave a short laugh. "He doesn't look woolly to me. And he certainly didn't sound it when they were talking to us earlier. He gives off an air of competence."

"Well, he can't be too competent if he thinks your father would hurt someone. Come on. We have to eat anyway," said Abby, turning towards the dining room. "Let's go have dinner. If we can sit next to them, fine. If not, we'll have a word when they leave."

"About what? We still don't know anything."

"About the family and all the connections."

"They know about the family. The problem is they don't think it has anything to do with Kelly's death."

Mandy was usually the positive thinker in the family. Abby didn't like the tone of negativity that was creeping into all her comments. Was she losing hope they could prove Richard's innocence? Or was she playing devil's advocate?

Chapter Eight

The dining room was long and narrow. The entryway to the kitchen bisected the room from the side, across from the main entrance. It wasn't very busy, so they had no difficulty getting a table in the area they wanted. They sat so that Abby was back-to-back with the sergeant. There were only a few tables occupied. Still, the low hum of conversation and the clattering of plates and cutlery meant that she couldn't make out the policemen's conversation.

They settled down to the business of dinner. Abby ordered a pasta dish with shrimp and garlic. "I love garlic," she said, "but it's not often you can eat it in public without offending someone. I promise not to breathe in the direction of your bed tonight."

Mandy ordered a curried lamb. The menu was nothing if not varied. There were steaks and chicken and a selection of burgers and even pizza as well as large seafood and pasta lists.

While they waited for their entrees, Abby sipped on a glass of white wine and Mandy a mineral water. Fortunately, neither of her children had gotten caught up in drinking during their teens. Abby and Richard had been relieved with the situation. Abby was pretty certain she had smelled alcohol on both of them at least once over the years, but it had only been a passing phase. *We are lucky in our children*, she

thought, glossing over the years of defiant screaming matches she had had with Mandy.

It wasn't long before Richard and his lawyer came into
the dining room. He took a quick look around the room,
acknowledged them with a brief smile and steered his companion in the direction of a corner table as far away from
them as he could get. Abby didn't blame him. It couldn't be
too comfortable trying to have a meal a few feet away from a
police detective who was accusing you of killing your fiancée.

The woman with Richard was tall and slim with straight
blonde hair falling to brush her shoulders. She looked to be
around forty, with a face of sharp planes that could be considered handsome rather than pretty. She had a firm set to
her mouth that seemed to say, "I'm all business." She carried a briefcase and wore a dark pantsuit with a lilac colored
blouse. Her whole appearance radiated confidence.

"Thank you, Mike," Abby breathed. To Mandy, she said,
"If appearances have anything to do with it, she's someone
who knows what she's doing."

"I bet she's a killer in a court room," said Mandy. Then
her face clouded, most likely realizing it might actually go
that far.

Abby reached out, putting her hand over Mandy's. "It
won't go that far. We, I mean they, the police, will find out
who really killed Kelly long before there's any trial or even an
arrest."

"I hope so, Mom. Dad looks as though he's happily in
control of everything, but a lot of it is just show. You've always been the strong one in the family."

Abby squeezed Mandy's hand again before letting it go.
"Funny, I never felt as though I was the one in control."

"Being in control and being strong aren't always the same
thing."

Abby noticed again Mandy's quick perceptions. She had
grown up so much in the past couple of years.

The dining room didn't get any busier. In addition to
Richard, his lawyer, the police and themselves, there were
only two more tables occupied. A family of four took one table, the two children, about eleven and thirteen, sat in a quiet, respectful manner she could never remember happening
when her children were that age. Again, the word control
slipped into the front of her mind.

She pulled her gaze away from the perfect family photo op and glanced at the occupant of the remaining table. A woman in a flowered caftan sat alone. She was probably in her late thirties with auburn hair of a shade that looked decidedly unnatural and a round pale face. She wore large rings on nearly every finger and chunky bracelets on both wrists. She was obviously a woman who wanted to make a statement with her appearance.

She looked up suddenly, and Abby wondered if she had felt that she was being watched. Then she realized the woman had looked up because she had company approaching her table. Mona Davenport and the woman they now knew to be Sylvia, her mother, took seats next to the woman in the floral caftan.

Abby poked Mandy. "Look, there, over to the right."

"It's Sylvia. And Mona."

"If that's the family dinner group, then Belinda must be the one in the caftan. She looks like you'd expect a medium to look. But maybe that's just for show."

"Are they the right age? The one in the caftan, Belinda, I guess, looks older than Kelly. And the daughters would have to both be younger."

"I think they are close in age. Kelly always took such care with her looks, which is probably why she looked younger. If Mona and Sylvia are eating together, who else could the other woman be, except Belinda? She certainly looks the part of a medium."

"Spa guest?" ventured Mandy.

"No, they'd be a lot chattier if they had a guest at the table. They're sitting together but not paying a lot of attention to each other. That looks like family to me."

"Is that what we do?"

"I didn't mean that in a bad way. I just meant families are comfortable together, so they don't have to talk all the time or put on a show."

"They're talking now," said Mandy. "Look."

And indeed, they were. Not in a friendly manner either. Belinda was gesturing, Sylvia looked close to tears, and Mona was speaking in low tones but with a tightly clenched jaw that suggested a disagreement

"Too bad we're not sitting closer to their table," said Abby.

"We wouldn't hear anymore there than we do from our

police friends." As Mandy spoke, the police both rose to their feet, ready to leave.

"Now," said Abby. "We have to talk to them before they go."

"I'm still eating," said Mandy. "So are you."

But Abby wasn't listening. "You stay here. I'm going to collar them in the lobby. I'll be back in a minute."

Chapter
Nine

She caught up to the police beside the reception desk, now empty. Jessie must have been done for the day.

"Excuse me, you're Detective...." Mandy had just told her his name a few minutes ago, but she hesitated, not wanting to give the impression she'd researched him.

"I'm Sergeant Woolly. And you are?"

"Abby Addison."

"Related to Richard Addison?"

"Yes, I'm his ex-wife. You've talked to my daughter."

"Yes." His gaze went to the dining room where the corner of the table that Mandy occupied was just visible.

"Were you here when it happened? I don't have you listed as a witness."

"No," said Abby. "I just got here."

"Do you have something new to tell us relevant to the case?"

"Not exactly," said Abby. "But I just wondered if you were aware of the family connections to Kelly here."

"We're aware."

"Then why are you so suspicious of Richard when surely Kelly's family has more to gain from her death than he does?" Abby was aware of her rising voice and forced herself to speak more calmly. "There is a lot of money involved in the family, I understand. Doesn't that make you wonder?"

"Except for the mother, they weren't even aware of who she was."

"And you believe that?"

"Until we find a reason not to."

"But what reason would Richard have to kill Kelly? They were going to get married. The fact that she found her birth mother wouldn't impact that at all. It doesn't make sense."

"Look, Ms. Addison." It was obvious Sergeant Woolly's patience was wearing thin. "We are following different lines of investigation and checking all information we have. No one has arrested your ex-husband, and we won't until we are sure we have evidence he did it."

"Until? Not if? It sounds to me as though you have your mind made up." Abby was not liking Sergeant Woolly at all.

"We do have evidence that links Mr. Addison to the crime. I'm sure everyone in the spa knows, so it doesn't hurt to tell you that we found his lighter at the scene, an unmistakeable lighter that he admits is his. Or, did you know that already?" His right eyebrow elevated in a question mark, but he didn't wait for her answer. "And they were overheard arguing."

"But anyone could have put that lighter there to implicate him. Richard says he lost it earlier in the evening at dinner."

"So he says." His lips clamped into a smile that Abby would have described as smug. He seemed a lot less inclined to take Richard's statements at face value than those of Sylvia.

"But why would Richard even be there? If he and Kelly were having a row, wouldn't it be more likely to have it in their room? Why go all the way to the downstairs treatment rooms to fight?"

"Why would anyone go there to fight?" scoffed Woolly. "That applies to anyone else you have in mind."

"And besides," piped up the taller policeman. "She wasn't coshed there. She was moved."

"That will do, Madison." Woolly gave his subordinate a long, hard look. Madison flushed but closed his mouth.

"She was killed somewhere else?" Abby was not going to let this go.

Woolly sighed. "Most of this is knowledge the whole staff has, and we've already had a newspaper sniffing around. Heaven knows what they've been told. I imagine you'll be able to read about it tomorrow anyhow, so I can tell you this.

She was drowned. It probably happened in the whirlpool. But the original attack began somewhere else, and she was moved. Now, *Miss Marple*, if you have nothing to add to the information we have, we're busy men."

If Woolly had been wearing a hat, Abby was sure he would have doffed it as he turned to leave. "But where? Where was she killed? Do you have the weapon that was used? Wh—" But Abby was talking to a retreating back.

She thought about his comment that everything he told her was public knowledge. Who had been talking to the press? Likely not the police. Any one of the spa staff who had been here at the time could have given the story out. Who would have known Kelly had been hurt somewhere else and lugged down the stairs to the whirlpool to drown? The picture that made in her mind was one she had to shake out. Poor Kelly! What a terrible way to die.

Then she stiffened in indignation as she remembered Woolly's reference to Miss Marple. How old did he think she was? She wasn't some elderly nosey woman in a shawl and lace gloves trying to ferret out a killer. She was trying to find out how to keep her ex-husband from being arrested for something he didn't do. Not the same thing at all!

She turned back to the dining room and sat down across from Mandy who gave her an inquiring look. Her daughter was sitting as she had left her. It didn't look as though she had eaten a bite of her meal since Abby had left.

Abby looked down at her own congealing food and pushed her plate aside impatiently.

"Well," said Mandy, "did you find out anything from the detective?"

"Other than the fact that he thinks of me as an eighty-year-old busybody?"

"What are you talking about?"

Abby shook her head. "Never mind. What I did find out is Kelly was originally hit somewhere else but it didn't kill her, and she was dragged down to the whirlpool where she was drowned."

"So what does that tell us?"

"It tells us that the original attack was probably a spur-of-the-moment rage, and then the attacker decided to finish the job."

"I'm surprised he told you all that."

"He didn't want to, but his sidekick blurted out some of the information. Apparently, someone here talked to the papers, so we should read about it in tomorrow's news. So he wasn't really giving away anything. I think he ended up telling me anything he thought would get rid of me."

"Well, at least they've gone without talking to Dad again. Maybe that's a good sign."

"Have they actually left the spa? Or did they go back to the office? I can't see from this angle."

"They left," said Mandy whose line of sight included the reception area. "There's no one at the office."

Richard and his lawyer took that moment to leave their table. As they passed Abby and Mandy, Richard gave them a short smile and a quick wave, mouthing "later." He didn't look as though his talk to his lawyer had cheered him up at all.

"I'm not hungry anymore," said Abby. "Are you?"

"No, let's go back to the room and see what Dad has to say."

"Wait, wait," said Abby, grabbing her daughter's hand to make her sit down again.

"What is it?"

"Sylvia is on the move. The other two are staying, but she's heading out. Let's follow her and at least find out what room she's in. Maybe we can even get a chance to talk to her." They signed their dinner bill quickly and left it on the counter and followed Sylvia out to the lobby.

But when they got there, there was no sign of her. The staircase was empty. She couldn't have climbed the huge flight that quickly. The office and reception area were still vacant.

"Where did she go?"

"She must have taken the elevator. Look. The light's on. Quick, up the stairs, and we'll see where she goes. They ran up, Abby puffing from the exertion, Mandy's younger body taking the flight easily.

"The elevator is still going," said Abby. "She must be on the third floor." Abby groaned.

By the time they got to the third floor, Sylvia's back was already turned to them as she walked down the hall. They hung back until she turned the corner to the right past the ice and drink machines. She followed through an archway, into another wing. It was above the treatment rooms. Of course, the apartments for staff were in a different section. Theo had told them that. Sylvia pushed her key card into a slot on the door marked 333S and paid them no attention as she entered her room.

Mandy said, "Should we talk to her now?"

"I don't think so," said Abby slowly. "In fact, I think we should separate."

"Why?"

"I think she'll open up more with one person. She might feel under attack if we both start to question her. Because I'm older, she might be a little more trusting of me."

Mandy looked as though she were going to protest.

Abby went on. "And I think your dad would feel more comfortable talking to you without my butting in. So, if you go see what your dad found out from his lawyer, I'll talk to Sylvia. Does that make sense to you?"

"I guess so."

Abby patted her on the shoulder and then pulled her hand back as she realized Mandy cold interpret it as a gesture of dismissal to a child. "We'll meet up back at the room and see if we're any further ahead."

Chapter Ten

Abby waited until Mandy was on her way down the stairs to knock on the door. She waited a moment and, not hearing any movement, knocked again, a little harder. Maybe Sylvia was in the bathroom. She heard a noise on the other side of the door that sounded like a muffled bark.

This time the door was flung open. Sylvia started to turn back into her room saying, "I told you I don't want to talk about..." Then she stopped, obviously just realizing it was a stranger in her doorway. She stared at Abby. "Who are you? You must have the wrong room." Her eyes looked damp, so barring any major allergy, she had been crying.

"I'm Abby Addison, and I wondered if I could talk to you for a minute."

"Oh, you're the one I saw at the desk earlier today. You were with the girl, the one who came with Kelly." She sniffled into a tissue she pulled out of her pocket. It looked already wet and used.

"Yes. I'm Mandy's mother. I want to talk about Kelly." Abby shifted her balance as though she were going to step forward. As she expected, Sylvia automatically took a step back, giving Abby the opportunity to slip in. Sylvia gave a shrug and backed up into the room, Abby right behind her.

Sylvia said, "I don't have anything to say about Kelly. I never got to meet her." A small white dog gave a short yap and came to investigate the visitor. Abby instinctively reached out her hand before considering the wisdom of making unauthorized overtures to a lap dog. This one seemed less yappy and friendlier than most she had met. It gave Abby's hand a sniff and went to stand beside its mistress. Sylvia reached down absent-mindedly to pat it.

"But you were her birth mother." Abby tried to keep her voice low. She didn't want to come across as censorious. "You were going to meet her later that night?"

"Yes." Short, terse answer.

"Where were you going to meet?"

"We were going to meet in the little anteroom before the rainforest. It's quiet and pleasant in there."

"So you went there expecting to see her."

"Yes."

"What did you do when she didn't show? What did you think had happened?"

Sylvia shrugged her right shoulder. "She could have changed her mind. People do."

"You did," said Abby, referring to Kelly's original request.

Sylvia seemed to know what she meant. "Yes. There were reasons I couldn't answer Kelly's request to meet earlier."

"Your husband?"

Sylvia looked as though she was going to deny it but slumped down into a chair and said, "Yes." Her right hand clenched the damp tissue so tightly her knuckles turned white.

Abby took the opportunity to also sit down, unbidden, in a chair across from her. Maybe the conversation would go better seated. "Your husband never knew about Kelly?"

"No." She sighed. They sat in silence for a moment before Sylvia seemed to decide talking was more comfortable than silence. "I was only sixteen when I had Kelly. My parents were very religious. They sent me away to stay with relatives during the pregnancy. When the baby came, they arranged the adoption. I didn't want to, but I was young." She looked lost in thought for a moment then went on. "I met Edward at our church. Our families had known each other for years, and we got married. My parents told me never to tell him, and I didn't. He would have never understood or forgiven."

"So you kept the secret for all your marriage?"

"You had to know Edward. There's no way he could have

lived with that knowledge without making my life unbeara-ble, more unbearable than it already was." She shrunk back into her chair.

"So you told the adoption agency no contact when Kelly tried to see you?"

"Yes. When she was born, I gave her a name. I called her Melody. That's how I've always thought of her, and it's hard now to call her Kelly." Tears welled in her eyes. "I wanted to see her. Oh, I really wanted to, but I couldn't."

"And then, when your husband died..."

"When Edward died, seeing Kelly was the first thing I thought of. I would be able to see my baby girl finally. Even with the horrible way he died, I couldn't dredge up any sym-pathy for him, husband or not. I'm sorry," she said, dabbing at her eyes with the now quite soaked bit of tissue. "That sounds terrible, but you had to know Edward to understand how I felt."

"Go on."

She reached over to the little table beside her chair and whipped out a fresh tissue, dabbing at her eyes again. "So I got in touch with the agency again to see if she still wanted to make contact. I didn't hear back for a while. I thought she had given up, or moved, or something. After all those years, I just had to see her. Then, finally, I heard back with a con-tact number. I called her and we arranged to meet here."

"Why here?"

"I wanted somewhere I would feel safe, somewhere near my other daughters."

Safe sounded like a strange word but there were all kinds of safety. Abby assumed she meant emotionally safety. "But you didn't tell them what was going on?"

"No, I was afraid to until I knew it was going to be all right. I wanted to be able to describe Melody—I mean Kelly—to them and have them looking forward to meeting her. Then we could all have our first Christmas together as a full family. I was afraid something would go wrong. And it did."

Sylvia made a motion as though she were going to get up, and Abby wanted her to stay seated. If she got up, the distance between them would increase, and the conversation would stop.

She rushed to say, "So the first thing Mona and Belinda knew of Kelly was in the morning when Richard went to the desk looking for her?" Abby hoped to create familiarity by using the family's first names. She didn't want Sylvia to freeze up. It seemed to work.

"Yes," Sylvia pulled out the tissue again, wiping it sideways under her eyes. "It was finally my chance to meet my eldest daughter, and now I'll never get to see her again. If only she hadn't..."

For a moment, Abby thought Sylvia had forgotten her presence. She stared off into the distance, her voice lowered as though her words were only for her own benefit. "If only she hadn't what?" Abby asked.

Sylvia straightened and put the tissue back in her pocket. "Nothing. I was just wishing I had a chance to meet her."

"I'm so sorry things turned out the way they did. I knew her. Of course, you know that."

"I thought she was going to marry your ex-husband."

"She was. Richard and I divorced long before he met her. She wasn't the cause of our breakup, and we got along quite well. We were becoming friends." A bit of a lie, thought Abby, but not really, because the last time they'd met Kelly had expressed that exact wish. Maybe she really hadn't meant it but...

"I'd waited so many years to make contact." Sylvia was becoming dreamy again. "Then, to have it all end without a chance to hold my baby ever again, a chance to stroke that beautiful hair, to see her smile with that precious dimple in her right cheek..."

Whoa, thought Abby.

Suddenly, Sylvia stopped talking and put her hand to her mouth.

"You said you never saw her," Abby accused. "It sounds as though you met her. Even if you saw a picture...that bit about the dimple... You did meet her!"

"Only for a minute." Sylvia grew agitated and confused. "I didn't mean to say that. Mona will be... She was alive when I left her." Her voice became increasingly louder, and Abby thought she was going to break down and give her a full account of her meeting when a key card sounded in the lock, and the door flung open. Mona stood in the doorway for a moment, the picture of an avenging angel, then shouted, "What are you doing to my mother? Get out of here. Now!"

Abby realized this was not a woman to argue with and

slid towards the doorway, "I'm sorry to have upset you, Sylvia," she said," but I needed to know."

"Now," said Mona, pointing to the doorway.

Abby had no choice.

"I'm sorry, Mona. She got me confused. I didn't say anything." Sylvia's voice was nearly a whimper.

Abby wondered if Sylvia had shed those years of subordination to her husband only to replace him with her daughter. And was Mona simply being overprotective of her mother, or did she have something to hide?

And then the door closed firmly on Mona's lowered, soothing sounds, and she could hear no more.

But it was true. Sylvia must have met Kelly. There was no mistaking that. And there was also no mistaking the fact that Mona knew and had told the family to keep quiet. Did Belinda and Jessie know, too? Was this a family conspiracy? But that was ridiculous, thought Abby. The silence was a conspiracy, but she couldn't see how Kelly's death could be.

She continued to think about the conversation as she took the stairs down to her room. Sylvia probably met Kelly in the rainforest waiting room as planned. Then what? Did they argue? Did Kelly leave then and meet her killer? Or, did Sylvia leave and someone who knew about the meeting came in and killed her there? If so, why there and why move her? That was the strange part. She wasn't dead when she was moved, because she drowned. The police had admitted that. Abby was determined to find the answers.

Chapter Eleven

When she got to the room, it was empty. Mandy must have still been with Richard. She slipped off her shoes and curled up in one of the easy chairs with her feet tucked up under her. She checked the coffee pot. It was empty. There was one packet of coffee there, and they would need that in the morning. She opened the door of the little bar fridge. There was still a few inches of white wine left in the bottle that sat in the door. She pulled it out and found a clean glass. The room seemed too quiet. Most people liked silence to think, but Abby always felt her mind worked better with white noise. She turned the television on and set the volume to low.

Then she stopped and stared at the screen. The channel was a local one, and the news was just finishing. There, on the screen, was a picture of Kelly with a wide smile, the one dimple showing in her right cheek. So maybe Sylvia could have seen it in a photo. But then, her reaction proved otherwise.

The news announcer said, "Police are still investigating the death." So no news there unless she had missed it. If only she had turned on the TV a few minutes earlier... They wouldn't know more than the police had told Abby anyway. The difference was that news journalists liked to give information. Police didn't.

The door jiggled as Mandy came back. She threw her purse and room key on the end of the bed. "Hi, Mom. How did things go with Sylvia?"

"I got interrupted just as I was starting to get information from her. Mona came charging to the rescue and shooed me out. But I'm pretty sure Sylvia actually met Kelly. I just don't know what happened afterwards." She told Mandy about the conversation and Mona's stormy arrival.

As she took a sip of her wine, she realized she was at the bottom of the glass. She decided against another. It was too late, and she needed to stay clearheaded.

"How is your father holding up?" she asked.

"About how you'd think. He's nervous as a cat and wanders around the room, picking things up and putting them down again. Then he scrolls through the e-mails on his phone, but I don't think he ever reads one. I doubt he's getting any sleep. He says the lawyer seems confident. Her name is Taylor H. Couling. She even sounds brilliant. Why do women with last names as their first always sound more intelligent than the Sallys and Susans?"

Abby took that as a rhetorical question and waited for Mandy to go on.

"Dad didn't have anything more to say. The lawyer doesn't want him to talk to anyone, even us, but he said there's nothing to say anyhow."

Abby and Mandy got ready for bed in near silence. The television hummed softly in the background, but neither was watching. Mandy had a bath. Abby decided to wait for a morning shower. She was too tired to do anything but sleep.

She snapped off the television as Mandy came out of the bathroom. "Night, love."

"Night, Mom."

Then the room fell quiet. Only the silence wouldn't stretch to the workings of Abby's mind. She went over every detail of what they knew. How did Richard's misplaced lighter get into the whirlpool room with Kelly? Had she borrowed it for some reason and forgotten to tell him? No, because a) she didn't smoke and b) she knew he was looking for it. Abby didn't think Kelly was the prank-playing kind, so she wouldn't have done it as a joke or a reprimand of his smoking. So how? She remembered one summer during college when she'd worked in a hotel. She'd been a room cleaner but the one thing she remembered about lost articles was that people reported them to the reception desk and the people who found them did the same. The hotel Abby had worked in had a complete closet in the back of the office for lost and found items. She would check tomorrow and ask Jessie if anyone had reported seeing the lighter. But of course, if they had, it would still be there, not with Kelly in the whirlpool room. *Think Abby!*

She refused to think of the other possibility. It was possible Richard was lying. She had been married to him long enough to recognize a lie when she heard it. Then she remembered the surprise she had felt along with the hurt when she had discovered his lies, so she couldn't count on her perception where her ex was concerned. Could someone have gone through the lost and found items and taken the lighter? No, that would have been remembered by staff. Abby rolled over, pulling the covers out of their snug fit around the mattress. Someone with access to the office could have slipped the lighter unobserved. Anyone at the spa would have that access—Mona, Sylvia, Belinda, or any of the staff.

Abby rolled over the other way. The covers bunched under her in an uncomfortable way, and she threw them to the foot of the bed. It was warm in the room. Should she get up and open a window or turn down the thermostat? Too much effort.

She rolled over again, pushing the covers down even further with her feet. Sylvia had seen Kelly. Why hadn't she told the police? Maybe she had, but they weren't telling anyone. Was the rainforest anteroom the place she was first attacked? And with what? Abby remembered the collection of smooth rocks worked into the décor. Most of them sat in little bowls but a few larger ones were part of a waterfall display. Maybe one of those was what knocked her out.

She had to talk to Sylvia again. Without Mona's presence. Sylvia either had to be the one to cosh Kelly, or she must have seen someone in the corridors, someone who took advantage of Kelly's state to finish the job. But why move her? Why not finish her off where she lay? The more Abby thought of it, the more she decided it had to be Sylvia. She was there. Abby could just about picture one person wanting Kelly dead, but two people in the same place? No, the person that coshed her had to be the same one who moved her to the whirlpool to drown her. But for some reason, they wanted her found there rather than the anteroom.

"You can't sleep?"

"Sorry, Mandy. Am I keeping you awake?"

"You mean because you're thrashing around like a hippo mid-stream? No, Mom, of course not." Abby could almost hear her grin. "I can't sleep either. I'm just a quieter non-sleeper than you are. Should we get up for a while and try again?"

"I don't think it would work."

"Neither is what we're doing now. I'm going to make some coffee."

"And you think caffeine will help us sleep? Count me in." Abby turned on a lamp and swung her legs over the bedside. She padded over to check the thermostat which was set at 72 degrees. She lowered it to 66. That should help a little. Abby never was able to sleep in a warm room.

"Of course, now we won't have coffee for the morning," said Mandy, "but we can hold out till we have breakfast."

The coffee finished burbling into the decanter and she poured two cups. They both drank it black.

"I was thinking about the lighter," Abby began. She told her all her thoughts about an employee slipping it out of the lost and found.

"The thing that kept my mind going around," said Mandy," was why hit her first and then drown her? It doesn't make any sense at all."

"And I can't see any reason for Sylvia to hurt her long lost daughter that she'd waited years to see," said Abby. "There's no motive there."

"There is for the rest of the family if they thought Kelly was going to get a big share of their inheritance. Maybe Sylvia was going to give her a big settlement to make up for all the lost years."

Abby rummaged in her purse and brought out an old notebook and pen. "Okay," she said. "We'll make a list. Who? How? Why?"

She started with Sylvia's name. "I don't see the why here. She was anxious to meet her daughter, so what possible reason could she have to kill her. The how is a little dicey, too. I can't picture Sylvia dragging Kelly all the way down to the whirlpool and drowning her there. I know she's not exactly elderly, but it just doesn't seem likely."

"Mona next," said Mandy. "We can see why for her. She

would be worried about all those lovely dollars going to a half-sister she'd never met. How is easy, too. She's young, strong, and determined. It would be easy for her to get Kelly down the hall."

"Belinda," said Abby. "The same applies to her for both why and how."

"Jessie?" Mandy suggested. "I wonder if she would be up for any of her great-aunt's money. They were awfully close, but without knowing what Sylvia has in her will, there's no use speculating."

Abby sighed and set down the pen. "There's not much use speculating about any of them. Sylvia seems to be in good health. Any money she's allocating in her will could be decades away. And we have no way of knowing her plans. Maybe she's going to give them all a payout from her husband's money." Then she brightened. "Maybe money has nothing to do with it. Maybe there's another motive."

"Like what?"

"Maybe she was in the wrong place at the wrong time and heard or saw something she shouldn't."

"That seems a little far-fetched. Does the spa look like a criminal haven for smugglers or drug cartels?"

"Looks can be deceiving. We're on the coast. There could be drug smuggling. I keep reading in the paper about boats being seized along the coast with a fortune in drugs onboard."

Mandy snorted. "I think you're really reaching."

"Well," said Abby crossly. "What do you think?"

Mandy thought a moment. "The spa isn't the type of hotel filled with young people out partying till all hours or late socials. But still, there should be the odd insomniac wandering the hallways in the evening. Why didn't anyone see anything?"

"Maybe they did but just didn't think it counted. After all, there are several residences here as well as the hotel rooms. If any of the occupants were seen wandering the hallway, it would seem perfectly normal."

"Hmm. Maybe. Back to the drugs. You said earlier you thought Theo was into steroids."

Abby shot down her own previous idea. "Maybe I was just being malicious because he looked too perfect and was making eyes at you."

Mandy gave a quick laugh. "Warn me not to bring boy-friends to see you."

Abby was going to comment on her daughter's love life, or lack of it, but decided it was not the right time. It probably never would be the right time. Instead, she said, "Even if he were on steroids, they aren't all that illegal, are they?"

"I don't know. I don't think you'd get into enough trouble to warrant killing someone over steroids to keep them quiet. Look at all the athletes that get caught using them. It's only a big deal because it's considered cheating, not because they're illicit."

"Okay, back to the family. The police say the rest of the family didn't know about Kelly. Sylvia says the same."

Mandy snorted. "I don't think the police are that naïve. I'm sure they're taking it with a grain of salt." She stopped for a moment and said, "I've been thinking. Maybe we're too pessimistic about this. We're afraid because they questioned Dad. What if they really believe him and are just letting everyone think he's their main suspect? They certainly aren't going to keep us in the loop. And they haven't arrested him."

"You're right," Abby set down her nearly empty coffee cup. "And on that positive thought, I'm going to try again to get to sleep. How about you?"

Mandy yawned. "You know, I think the coffee worked. Sometimes things have an opposite effect. I'm sleepy now."

So was Abby. She fell into a dreamless sleep almost immediately.

Chapter Twelve

Abby awoke to a dark room, wondering if it was morning yet. She was used to getting up in the night at least once for a bathroom trip, and last night she had downed both coffee and wine. It was December, so lack of light was no indicator. The bedside clock faced Mandy. Abby scrambled her hand along the table until she found her watch. The luminous dial showed it was just after seven. By the time she'd made her trip to the bathroom, Mandy was stirring.

"Do you want to go before I shower?" asked Abby.

"Okay," Mandy yawned. "I'll just be a moment."

While she waited, Abby drained the last couple of table-spoons of coffee from the carafe into her mug and slipped it into the microwave for a few seconds. It tasted horrible, but at least it was enough caffeine to last her until breakfast.

She showered. Abby was all dressed and ready to go by the time Mandy appeared from the bathroom in a long terry robe, a white towel wrapped around her hair.

"You are an addict," said Mandy, laughing at her mother's impatience for breakfast. "Why don't you go ahead and have your coffee first. I'll join you for breakfast in about ten minutes."

Abby didn't argue. Maybe she needed to cut down on her caffeine. It was a drug, after all, and she didn't like some-thing controlling her. The last time she'd decided to cut her coffee, she'd foolishly done it cold turkey. By noon of her first day without, she'd been doubled over with nausea and a migraine-like headache. When she realized it was the result of caffeine withdrawal, she'd quickly gulped a cup of coffee and the symptoms disappeared almost immediately. She would try again, but in a more moderate way.

But not this week. She had too much on her mind to want to fuzz it with lack of a stimulant.

Breakfast was cafeteria-style. She took her coffee and then, deciding she was hungry as well, filled a plate with scrambled eggs, a slice of Canadian bacon and toast. She added a small cream cheese tub to her tray and sat down by a window table.

She looked around to see if there was any sign of Sylvia or her daughters, but the other tables were either empty or occupied by couples she didn't recognize. She had nearly finished her plate when Mandy walked in. She pointed to the table to indicate she'd already had hers, and Mandy headed for the line of warmers.

She came back with a more judicious choice—no eggs or bacon, just a plate of strawberries, melon, pineapple, and a whole grain muffin.

Abby made a face. "Trying to show me up?"

"I'm sure your doctor will let you know when your blood turns to grease, but I actually don't like bacon or eggs. I never did, if you remember."

"Hmm. I should try a more healthy diet, and I will, just not this week. I need my energy."

"Not many people around." Mandy scanned the room as Abby had done.

"We could have called your dad to see if he wanted to join us."

"I thought of it, but it's still early, and he might be sleeping."

"He never eats breakfast anyway, just coffee. You're right. We'll let him be until he calls us."

Abby brought up the idea of the lighter and lost and found again. "One of us should say we lost something and ask to look."

"What good would that do us? The lighter isn't there now, and we have no way of knowing if it ever was."

"Maybe they keep a log of items."

"Hmm. Could be. But they wouldn't show us that."

"I'm going to give it a try anyhow. We have to do something. We can't just sit around. I'll meet you back in the room." She finished her second cup of coffee and pulled off one of her earrings, shoving it into her purse.

Jessie was at her post at the reception desk. She looked up warily as Abby approached. "Can I help you?" she asked, but her heart didn't seem to be in the question.

"I wonder if I could check your lost and found," said Abby. "I seem to have lost an earring, and I wonder if someone found it and turned it in."

"I don't think so," said Jessie, not moving.

"Could you check your list for me to be sure?"

Jessie pulled a scribbler from a desk drawer with seeming reluctance and flipped it open. "When did you lose it?'

"Probably last night," she said.

"Didn't you have it when you put them on this morning?" Jessie asked the obvious question, probably suspicious of Abby's motives. Then why was she suspicious if there was nothing to hide?

"I forgot to take them out last night, so it could have fallen out then or this morning."

She tried to peer over Jessie's shoulder, but she screened her view of the book. She did get a passing glimpse of the page. It wasn't very neat and was written or printed in more than one hand, but Abby was pretty sure there had been an empty line towards the end of the page. It looked as though it had been filled in with white out.

Jessie slammed it shut and said, "No, no earrings at all. Maybe it will turn up in your bed if you slept in them." She turned in dismissal back to her computer. "Is there anything else?"

"No." Abby wished she could think of another reason to stay and talk to the reluctant Jessie, but she couldn't.

"I'll call your room if it turns up." Jessie's tone indicated she was sure it wasn't going to turn up.

Abby started up the long staircase and turned to look back at the desk after her first step. Jessie jumped to attention as she did, but not before Abby caught the puzzled frown on her face.

Chapter Thirteen

Just before she turned back to climb the stairs, Belinda appeared at the top of the flight. She was wearing a full length denim skirt with a long crocheted sweater. The effect was more hippie than fortune teller.

As Abby was about to speak to her, she stopped on the step above her and said, "You're the ex of the one who killed that girl, aren't you?"

"I'm the ex of the man who's accused of killing Kelly. He didn't do it. And 'that girl,' as you called her, was your sister," Abby said indignantly.

"Half-sister, you mean," said Belinda. "But no matter. Have you had breakfast?"

"Yes," said Abby," but I could do with another coffee." She assumed the question was an invitation.

"Come on then," said Belinda, sweeping past her.

They sat in a far corner of the dining room. No one else was around except for one couple who sat by the window, staring out at the view.

Belinda had loaded her plate with two toasted bagels, slices of cheese and a variety of fruits. She also had in reserve a cinnamon bun sitting in a pool of warm butter and a tall glass of orange juice.

On closer inspection, Belinda looked younger than Abby had first assumed. Her face was devoid of make-up, an unusual pairing with her gaudy jewellery. Her skin was unlined except for a slight crinkle on the side of each eye. She would probably be the younger of the two girls, judging from the older child syndrome Mona displayed. Abby guessed she was several years younger than Kelly had been. She saw little similarity in Belinda's looks to either Kelly or Mona. On the other hand, she could see a similarity between Mona and Kelly. It was around the eyes. Belinda probably took after her father, in appearance anyway, certainly not in personality. Mona was her daddy's girl, Abby surmised from what she had been told about Edward.

"So," Belinda said, "have you known Kelly long?" She bit into one of the bagels which she had topped with strawberry jam, and it began to ooze down her chin. She picked up a napkin and dabbed at it fiercely.

"I didn't know her well, but I met her over a year ago. When did you find out she was your half-sister?"

"The morning she was found dead. Didn't the others tell you?" Belinda's eyes held Abby's as though daring her to disagree. Abby wasn't going to. At least not yet.

"It seems rather strange that your mother arranges a meeting with Kelly, and the rest of the family doesn't seem to know about it."

"Oh we suspected something was going on," said Belinda with a grin. "Mona was beside herself wanting to know what it was, but in spite of Mother's cowed attitude, she can be amazingly stubborn at times."

"From what I've seen of Mona, she doesn't look like the type to give up easily. I'm surprised she admitted defeat." said Abby.

"So was I," said Belinda. She smiled again, and Abby wondered why she seemed to find the whole situation amusing.

"Did you see Kelly when she checked in?"

Her eyes shifted to the food arrayed on the table before she answered. "I don't think so. I don't usually pay much attention to the guests until they ask for my services."

"What exactly are your services?"

"I've always had a gift," Belinda said. "Ever since I was a child. I have the ability to see things in a different way from other people." Belinda took on a dreamy other-worldly expression, and Abby wondered if she really believed in her "gift," or if it was a well-rehearsed response to any observers. Abby wasn't a supporter of spiritualism but was willing to concede that the human mind had many facets that needed to be explored.

"So you're a medium?"

"Of sorts. I also read cards and leaves, whatever they want me to do. I'd love to do a reading for you. I wouldn't even charge you."

Abby didn't want to get side-tracked. "Maybe later, when this is all sorted out." She steered the conversation back to where it had been derailed. "What did you think when you first heard your mother had a daughter she gave up for adoption?"

"I thought she was cleverer than I gave her credit for."

"For having a baby?" Belinda seemed to be the odd man out in this serious family.

"No, for keeping it a secret from my father. He never liked people to keep secrets from him. I'm amazed she managed for so long."

"She never hinted to either of you? When you were adults?"

"No. She couldn't have done that. Mona would have tried to convince her to come out in the open and tell Dad. Mona always was Daddy's little girl. She wouldn't have let mother have any peace till she owned up."

"And you? Maybe your mother would have felt more comfortable confiding in you."

"Me? Oh, no one ever tells me secrets. I'm no good at keeping them." Belinda sounded as though she considered this to be an attribute. "Why are you here, if the man is your ex? What does it have to do with you?"

Abby was aware of another couple seating themselves nearby in her periphery, but they were far enough away to not put a dampener on the conversation.

"My daughter asked me to come. She was concerned her father was being blamed for something he didn't do."

"Maternal feelings have a funny way of causing action, don't they?"

"You said none of you knew about Kelly till the morning, but when I talked to Sylvia—"

"Mona let you do that?" Belinda looked at her incredulously.

"She wasn't there," said Abby. "Anyhow, Sylvia let something slip that showed she did see Kelly that night. Did you know about that?"

"She actually said that?"

"As well as. She said Kelly was alive when she left her at the rainforest room."

"Well, there you go. Mother has her faults, but she usually doesn't lie."

"But, if she saw her that night, she would have told you, wouldn't she? You must have known."

"Oops! Battleship approaching at three o'clock." Belinda popped a chunk of the cinnamon bun into her mouth.

Abby turned to see Mona descending on them.

Mona marched directly towards their table, arms swinging, frown fixed firmly on her brow and lips clenched so tightly that she must have been grinding her teeth. "I thought I told you to stay away from my family." She scowled at Abby.

"I'm sorry," said Abby, "but I thought you told me to leave your mother in peace, and I understand that. She's a bereaved mother and you want to protect her. You made no mention of the rest of your family. Besides," she said, casting a quick glance at her coffee companion, "I was invited to coffee."

"That's true." Belinda piped up, raising her hand like a schoolgirl being brought to account. "I did invite her."

Abby and Belinda both stared at Mona with a "so there" look, waiting for her response.

"I know you find this amusing," she said, looking at her sister, "but it isn't. Someone has been killed on our premises." She turned her frown to Abby who tried to look shamefaced, because she had been feeling amused at Mona's anger. "Mother is very upset, and I don't want outsiders talking to her. I don't want outsiders talking to any of the family. That includes Jessie."

"She's your receptionist! How can I avoid seeing her or talking to her?"

"Try harder." She sighed and made a quick transition to a more accommodating approach. "I'm sorry for your loss, Ms. Addison, and I'm sorry for the way it seems to be turning out, but my family is not involved, and I want to keep it that way. I would appreciate your discretion and cooperation."

"How can you say your family isn't involved? Kelly was

your family! You, more than anyone, should want to see the killer found."

"I trust the police to do their job. I'm sure they have their sights set on the culprit already. It's just a matter of letting them get on with their job and make an arrest."

"If you're talking about Richard," said Abby indignantly. "You're off the track completely. He loved Kelly and was going to marry her. He had no reason to want her dead."

"Then why were they fighting just before she died? And why was his lighter found beside her?" She made a half-turn away. "I'm sorry, but I don't wish to discuss this anymore. I only want you to leave the family alone. My family, that is."

"I don't see how you can feel this doesn't concern you. It does. Your mother did see Kelly."

"Did she tell you that? I talked to her after your conversation, and I don't think she said anything of the kind. Because it isn't true." The last sentence was added as though an afterthought.

"She just as much as admitted it, and she would have if you hadn't interrupted."

Mona actually smiled. "Then it's a good thing I interrupted, isn't it?" The smile turned into a smirk.

"I know your mother saw Kelly before she died, and I know the rest of you knew about her that night, whatever you say. I'm going to talk to the police and tell them just that. You and your mother have been lying about what happened. You may be able to keep your mother from telling me the truth, but I don't think your tactics will work with the police. When they know what questions to ask, I'm sure Sylvia will tell them everything."

"I don't think you'd be wise to do that," said Mona. "Things may not turn out exactly as you think they will." And, with that cryptic comment, she motioned to Belinda to follow her out. Belinda did as she was told, but made a slow process of it, stopping to wrap the rest of her cinnamon bun in a napkin and stuffing it into her purse.

Then she stood and followed, but not before giving Abby a parting look and mouthing the words, "I'll talk to you later."

As they left the dining room, Abby could hear Mona asking in a low growling voice, "What did you say to her?" She didn't hear Belinda's answer.

What a strange family. Abby had thought her own family

was slightly unusual at times, but they had nothing on the Davenports—an overbearing and possibly abusive father who died in a "horrible" way, a mother who was submissive in everything except keeping her secret, and sisters with strange undercurrents simmering beneath the surface. Did Belinda resent the way Mona assumed their father's dominant role? If so, why go into partnership with her? Abby would have liked to be a fly on the wall of Sylvia's room, because that was almost certainly where these two were headed now for a family powwow.

Abby was positive that she was right. Sylvia had seen Kelly, and the rest of the family knew about her that night, not the next morning. But that raised a new question. Why did they lie? Had Abby been wise in telling them she knew about their lies and planned to tell the police? Mona's response to that had come across sounding like a threat. But what could she do? Abby shuddered. She felt as though someone were walking across her grave. Maybe she should have waited to see what the police were planning next. As usual, she dove right in without a plan, without thinking of the consequences. The difference was, this time, the consequences would not be hers to face. They were Richard's.

Chapter
Fourteen

Abby set aside her coffee, grabbed her purse, and went upstairs. She wondered if Mona might ask her to leave the spa. That would be a problem. She would have no contact with any of the staff or family. But it would be one way for Mona to keep her ineffective. On the other hand, Mona might feel better knowing she could keep an eye on her. She had a problem getting her family to follow orders. Abby had the feeling she wasn't used to being crossed.

Mandy was stretched out on her bed, watching a rerun of *Friends* on television. Her eyes were half-closed, and Abby was pretty sure, if asked, she wouldn't have been able to describe the plot.

"Sorry if I woke you," said Abby plopping down at the foot of the other bed.

"I wasn't sleeping, only killing time till you got back. Did it take you that long to check lost and found?"

"Nothing in lost and found about a lighter, but from what I could see of the book, there was an entry whited out near the end of the last page. And Jessie went out of her way to keep me from looking at it."

"Maybe she's just trained to keep customers, or do they call us guests, from looking at confidential information."

"What's confidential about lost items? Anyhow, that wasn't what took up my time. Belinda was coming down the stairs as I was leaving reception and invited me to have breakfast with her, well, coffee."

That got Mandy's attention, and she sat up with sudden interest. "Mona allowed her to talk?"

"Not for long."

"What's Belinda like?"

"Not like the rest of the family. Maybe she's a changeling. Mona seems to take after her father, and Sylvia allows her to walk over her the way she must have done with her husband. Belinda, well, she just seems to go along with everything when she feels like it and does her own thing when she doesn't. For some strange reason, she seems to be enjoying herself."

"Did she offer to read your tea leaves?"

"I wasn't drinking tea. I was drinking coffee."

"I was being facetious, Mom. Did she come across as you'd expect a medium to?"

"I'm not too sure what I expected a medium to be like, but it definitely wouldn't be Belinda. Oh, she did talk about her 'gift' in a remote sort of way, but there's nothing ethereal about her. And she may not have offered to read my tea leaves, but she did ask to do a reading for me. I'm not sure what kind of a reading she meant. Maybe it was tea leaves."

"So, other than drumming up business, did she have anything interesting to say?"

"She wasn't drumming up business. She offered to do the reading for free. The conversation was just starting to get interesting when Mona came charging up to the table."

"Uh-oh."

"Uh-oh, indeed." Abby related her conversation with Mona and watched Mandy's face take on a startled look. "You don't approve of the way I handled it?"

"It's not that I disapprove, exactly. Mom, it's just..."

"Come on. Out with it. You never used to have trouble telling me when I was in the wrong. What are you worried about?"

"This is a little different than a disagreement about curfew, Mom, and I'm not even sure why I'm worried. I think maybe we don't know enough about Mona to know how she's going to handle this."

Abby sighed deeply and then began to pace the room, touching each piece of furniture as she rounded the room. "I know, I know. When I left the dining room, I felt as though I'd made a mistake, too. I'm not sure what it was, but I didn't like Mona's last comment about things not turning out the way I thought they would."

"You've always been good at upsetting apple carts, Mom."

"The trouble is this may affect your father. I wonder what she'll do now." Abby talked as she continued to pace, speaking more to herself than to Mandy. "She nearly has to go to the police now. They'll have a family conference and decide what to tell them. They'll work out a story that explains why they lied to begin with. They can't risk us going to the police first. It will look so much more believable if they get there first. Damn! That's what I should have done!"

"What?"

"I should have shut my mouth and gone straight to the police. Then they would have been caught in the lie and would have blundered around, trying to explain. Now, it's us that's caught flat-footed."

"Maybe it doesn't matter who tells them, just that they know the family did get to meet Kelly."

"You're changing your tune."

"I don't have a tune to change, Mom. I honestly don't know if this will help or hurt Dad."

"Then let's spike their guns. Let's go talk to the police before they get a chance to."

"I'm with you."

"Are you going to call Dad, and tell him what we're doing?"

Mandy hesitated. "No, I don't think so. He'd remind us the lawyer told us not to get involved."

They grabbed their purses and coats, and Mandy searched for the car keys. They passed the front desk on their way out, and there was no sign of Jessie. Maybe it was too close to Christmas Day to have anything for reception to do. The spa seemed to have thinned out, judging from the number of people they had seen in the dining room. They followed the hall to the parking lot exit at the rear of the building, and Mandy pointed to a car just leaving the lot.

"Look. Isn't that Mona at the wheel?"

Abby squinted and said, "Looks like her. And there are four people in the car. They must be going to make their confession."

"I don't think it's going to be a confession. I think it's going to be a setup to point all the blame at Dad."

"But what more can they say? If they had evidence they would have said so before now, I think they're just trying to cover their own behinds."

"Well, there's not much sense trying to race them. They have a head start."

"And they've probably phoned Sergeant Woolly ahead of time to say they're coming." Abby stopped short, and Mandy bumped into her. Abby turned and went back through the parking lot door to the spa with Mandy following.

"That's it!" she said. "We'll call Woolly and tell him what we know. Then he'll see that they're just doing a cover-up. Hurry up." She pulled at Mandy's sleeve. They ran up the stairs, and Abby pulled out a phone book. "Where do you find the police number? We can't use the emergency one."

"At the front."

"Here it is." Abby dialed and asked to be connected to Sergeant Woolly. A moment later, she put down the phone with a tsk of disgust.

"He's not there?" asked Mandy.

"He's tied up in a conference, they said. Did I want to leave a message, they asked."

"Do you think you should have left one?"

"When I asked for his partner, they said he was tied up, too. I don't think they would have answered any message I left."

"Well, it's a good sign, isn't it? They're not talking to the Davenports yet. It'll take them at least fifteen minutes to get there. So they must have other people they're interviewing. And, since Dad is still here, it can't be him. So it's a good thing."

"I hope you're right. I'm sure you are. But the more I think about my conversation with Mona, the worse I feel."

"Should we go tell Dad about it now?"

"No sense worrying him. It may all turn out for the best yet. I'm going to go for a walk. I want to clear my head."

"I'll come, too. I could do with some fresh air."

Chapter Fifteen

This time, when they walked through the lobby, a tall distinguished-looking man with gray hair was at the reception desk. Following close behind him was a shorter man, also impeccably dressed, but without the haughty air of the first. His ginger hair was slightly disheveled, and he took a swipe with a freckled hand to push it back into place. No Jessie, of course, but Tillie from the gift shop was doing double duty and gave them a key.

"I wonder who they are," said Abby.

"Why? There are other guests here, you know, apart from our family and the Davenports. It could be anyone."

"I don't think so. Look at Tillie."

Tillie was staring at the men's retreating backs as they headed for the elevators. Then she looked up at Abby and Mandy and put her hands over her ears, and then over her eyes. "It has to be Jessie's grandfather. Tillie wouldn't react that way to anyone else. And that gesture means they're the 'hear no evil' and 'see no evil' of the monkeys."

"Maybe you're right." They changed course and made for Tillie—the fountain of information.

"Is that who we think it is?" asked Abby smiling.

"Jessie's grandfather, Arthur. And the one with him is see no evil, Jack. I knew Arthur would show up just to see who would dare to commit a murder on his property." She flashed a grin, put her hand to her mouth, and said, "Oh sorry. That wasn't a very good way to put it. I didn't mean to..." The talkative Tillie seemed to flounder momentarily, but Abby and Mandy assured her they weren't offended. "I've got to get back to the shop," she said. "With Jessie gone, there's a bell to ring here at the reception desk that comes through to the gift shop so I can fill in for her." Abby and Mandy followed in her trail as she went back to her own duties.

"Is it Jessie's day off?" Abby inquired innocently, knowing full well where she was.

"No," said Tillie as she unlocked the shop door. "She went off somewhere with the rest of the family."

"Not family problems, I hope?"

"Honestly, I don't know where they've gone. They didn't say, but all four of them headed out in the same car. I watched them go out the drive."

"Well, I hope everything is okay. At least no one was suddenly ill, if they were all in the car," said Abby. It didn't look as though Tillie would be providing them with any new information.

"No, I guess not. Oh well, we'll find out soon enough. Old Arthur 'hear no evil' will be setting things in motion. He wasn't too pleased about the family being gone when he arrived. Although I don't see how he can be that upset when he didn't tell them he was coming. Good thing we had vacant rooms, or he'd be staying with Jessie, and she wouldn't like that too much."

"Jessie and her grandfather Arthur don't get along?" Abby scanned the counter of souvenir mugs as she questioned Tillie, hoping the browsing would take the edge off the inquisition and inspire more confidences.

"No, they've never gotten along. I think it's mostly because of the way he treats his sister, Sylvia. Jessie idolizes Sylvia and gets really upset because Arthur puts her down all the time. He's so much like his brother-in-law in that way."

"I imagine Jessie must have seen a lot of her great-aunt growing up to become that attached to her."

"Oh yes, she used to spend nearly all her summers there as a child. Her parents are academics. They spend their summers going on world tours and to conferences and heaven knows what else. Poor Jessie got dumped with her great-aunt a lot. I shouldn't say poor Jessie, I guess. I know she loved her summers there. Edward was usually busy, so she and Sylvia got to spend most of their time alone together."

"You must have known the family for a long time."

"Oh yes, that's why Mona gave me the job. I used to live on the same street as Sylvia and Edward. My husband was a good friend of theirs."

"Oh." For some reason, Abby hadn't pictured Tillie as a married woman.

From her little laugh, Abby realized Tillie was aware of the surprise.

"I wasn't married to Charles that long," said Tillie. "He decided his secretary had more curves than I did and took off with her to some tropical paradise. I haven't heard from him in decades." She took a breath and went on. "That's partly why the family kept up with me. Edward and Arthur were both very righteous men and thought Charles had behaved abominably. Edward gave me a job when I had to sell the house and move to an apartment. Charles left quickly but took all the money with him, and I never could track him down. I don't even know if I'm divorced or married." She smiled brightly. "I might even be a widow."

Abby wondered how much anger seethed beneath the bright smile. "I imagine you have reason to be grateful to the family."

Tillie let out a little sigh. "I guess so. It was nice of them to give me a job, but Edward wasn't an easy man to work for. And I always felt as though I was on sufferance and had to express my undying gratitude for his benevolence every day. I was glad, years later, when I got a chance to move on. It felt like real freedom to work for someone who actually smiled at you in the morning. I know how Sylvia must feel now—free at last—even if it was a rather horrible way to get out from under her husband."

Abby didn't say anything, but it didn't look as if Tillie had really moved on. She was back working for a Davenport again, a different Davenport, but still in hock to the family. The family seemed to have a magnetic pull that brought people into their circle and wouldn't set them free. Maybe that explained why Tillie was so quick to pass on all their dirty laundry to near strangers. Maybe it was her way of feeling as though she had some control. The question was, were the Davenports aware of Tillie's indiscreet words? Maybe they just ensured she never knew anything of real importance to divulge, or maybe they were just so self-centered that they never thought to be concerned.

"If Sylvia didn't like her marriage, surely she could have divorced him," Abby said.

"Divorce Edward? You must be mad. He wouldn't have allowed it. Sylvia was under his thumb, and the only thing that got her out from under was his death. That was certainly a gift from the gods, if you could say that about dying in such an awful way."

The telephone rang and Abby couldn't think of a valid reason to remain standing around the gift shop. She exchanged a questioning look with Mandy, and they both turned to leave. Abby had forgotten all about her wish to go for a walk to clear her head and so, apparently, had Mandy.

They climbed the stairs wordlessly and each flopped tiredly on the edge of a bed. Abby had never felt so discouraged. She had answered her daughter's plea for help, hoping she would be able to do something constructive, but any efforts on her part had just made things worse.

She thought back to the last time she'd been faced with death. At the request of her old friend Nikki she'd flown off to a private island on Lake of the Woods. She had been able to unmask a killer, but not before nearly being killed herself. She shuddered at the memory of standing face-to-face with a cold-blooded murderer. She hoped Kelly had never seen the blow coming. Thinking of last summer turned her thoughts to Neil, the one good thing that came out of the experience, aside from saving Nikki's life, of course. Neil was a part of Nikki's entourage, her lawyer actually, and Neil had been part of her escape from death. She wondered if she should call him, then remembered his itinerary. He would likely be in the air now somewhere between Toronto and Turks and Caicos. One part of her ached to be with him, but another more important part knew she had to see this through for her daughter's sake, if not for her ex-husband's. She would call Neil tomorrow.

She sighed and blinked back tears. Why hadn't she just relied on the police to settle things? That's what they are trained for. *Because the police sometimes get it wrong.* Nikki had gone to the police when she'd thought someone had been trying to kill her, but they'd just written her off as a hysterical woman. And this Sergeant Woolly, he thought Richard could be a killer and didn't seem inclined to look elsewhere. She had the advantage. She knew Richard, had been married to him for twenty plus years, and she knew he couldn't kill someone. The police didn't have that knowledge.

She sat up. She couldn't stand the four walls of this room any longer. "I'm going for that walk now," she said. This time Mandy didn't offer to join her.

Chapter Sixteen

Abby went out the back way, through the parking lot. She didn't see the car back yet, the one the Davenport clan were in. Ether they had to wait to see Woolly, or it was a long interview. What could they be telling him? Probably everything they thought Abby might leak to them. They wanted to appear to be forthright and cooperative. Abby just hoped there wouldn't be any surprises in their revelations. She should have held her tongue and just ignored Mona instead of goading her into retaliatory action.

That little voice in her head—the one that popped up to speak its mind in the most unpleasant situations—decided to have its say. Abby shook her head, trying not to listen, but the thoughts came anyway. Was it possible her resentment towards Richard had simmered over into her actions and made her not as cautious as she should have been in her dealings with Mona? Had some evil part of her deliberately sabotaged the situation? No. She refused to consider the possibility. She felt lingering bitterness towards Richard and still hadn't forgiven him for his unfaithfulness, but nothing would cause her, even subconsciously, to put him in danger. Besides, it was Mandy she came to help and support. She shook herself free of doubts, like a dog shedding a coat of snow. She looked down at her feet, clad in loafer-type shoes rather than the boots she should have worn. Her toes were beginning to feel the cold.

Snow started falling in huge, soft flakes. "It's beginning to look a lot like Christmas" played in her mind. She only wished it would begin to feel like Christmas. Tomorrow night would be Christmas Eve. Richard, Kelly, and Mandy should have been all together enjoying this holiday getaway. Abby should have been on her way to Turks and Caicos to have a romantic Christmas with Neil. Why did life always have to throw a spanner in the works?

There were walking trails around the spa, but Abby didn't have the proper shoes on, and she didn't feel like walking alone in the forest with a murderer in their midst. Besides, the light was dimming already. Night came early. The shortest day of the year had just passed a few days ago.

As she reached the parking lot, she saw the Davenport car. A figure appeared from behind a SUV, holding a leash with a small white dog at the other end. In her other hand, she held a small, brightly colored bag. Sylvia. The little dog pulled at the leash, trying to greet Abby. Apparently, it held no hard feelings towards Abby for upsetting his mistress earlier. She held out her hand. The dog seemed to approve of her smell, wagging its tail and most of its body.

"That's enough, Isis," said Sylvia.

Isis was a rather grand name for such a wee dog. Still, Abby wasn't one to judge. She had named her cat Ajax, after all. "You're back," she said, not able to think of a more creative comment.

"Yes. Just now. The others are going to dinner."

Sylvia pulled her shoulders up against the cold and gazed around the parking lot before looking back to Abby. "Look," she began, "it wasn't my idea to go today, to the police station, I mean. Mona was angry about your interfering and was afraid we'd get caught up in the situation."

Abby bit her tongue to stop herself from saying they were already caught up in it, but she knew she had to learn to stop blurting out unpleasant observations that merely put other people's hackles up. Instead, she said, "I should have been more careful in what I said to Mona, but I know Richard had nothing to do with Kelly's death."

Sylvia sighed. "You're probably right. But he's the only one outside of the family with any connection to her, so Mona thought we should circle the wagons. The rest of us usually go along with what she decides."

Abby sensed a certain sadness in her tone and felt a pang of sympathy. Sylvia hadn't had much of a life, living with a domineering man and unable to acknowledge her firstborn daughter. Now, she had lost her daughter before she had really found her. And her relationship with Mona seemed a little outside the normal mother-daughter bond.

"What exactly did you tell the police?"

"We told them about my relationship with Kelly and how we planned to meet."

"But you had already told them all that."

"Yes, but I hadn't told them I had actually met her and talked to her."

Abby straightened. Her depression over the results of her interference began to lift. Surely, when the family admitted to lying, it would put anything else they said into suspicious territory.

Sylvia went on. "They seemed to understand why I hadn't admitted it before. It was true, you know, that I never told my family about Kelly. They had no reason to hurt her. They didn't know who she was."

"Ah, but how did they react when they found out that night?" asked Abby.

"It wasn't until after I'd met Kelly..." her voice trailed off.

"When did you actually tell them Sylvia?"

Sylvia looked around her guiltily, glancing upwards at the windows on the top floor. "I can't talk to you here," she said. "I'm going in to have dinner with the others. Then I'll go to my room early. Belinda says I should tell you what happened. She says it's not right what Mona made us say."

"What did she make you say?"

"Not here," she repeated. "Come to my room at ten. No one will come to check on me after that, because I usually go to bed by then. Belinda will be there, too. We'll tell you what went on. Belinda says you should come by yourself. She thinks it will be more comfortable without your daughter there." Sylvia bunched the words together as though they had been rehearsed, and they probably had.

What a strange family, thought Abby, again. If one daughter wasn't telling Sylvia what to do, the other was. In the end, Belinda probably had the greater pull, Abby thought. Sylvia would follow Mona's lead outwardly but would probably go her own way when she could. Belinda, on the other hand, had a much softer approach, and there seemed a greater bond between the two, probably from years of circumventing orders together from the more dominant family members.

Sylvia turned quickly and pulled gently at the dog's lead. She disappeared around the outline of another large vehicle, and Abby saw her on the other side, stopping to deposit a small bag in the trash can before entering the rear of the hotel.

Abby reversed directions, followed the pathways around the side of the annex, and entered through the front entrance. Tillie was busy on the phone, but looked up to wave at her as she passed.

When she opened the door, Mandy was stretched out full-length on the bed, lying face up with silent tears coursing down her cheeks.

Chapter
Seventeen

"Mandy?" Abby crossed quickly to the bed. "Has anything else happened?"

Mandy sat up, and the tears were joined by audible sobs. "Oh Mom, I went to see Dad. Just as I got to the door, he came out." She stopped and grabbed a tissue from the bedside table before continuing. "There were two policemen with him, and they took him downstairs. They shooed me away and wouldn't let me talk to him."

"Woolly and his friend were here?"

"No, it was two other men."

"Were they arresting him?"

"They wouldn't say anything, just said I'd find out when they were ready to tell me."

"We'll have to phone his lawyer. What's her name?"

"I'll call," said Mandy. "I don't think she was too happy with you last time you talked. Dad had her card in his room. I have his spare key. I'll go and make the call from there."

Abby watched her go and then sat on her bed, scrunching the pillows behind her so that she could sit comfortably. Mandy seemed to want to make the call by herself, but Abby wished she had gone along. It was only a few minutes longer when she heard Mandy fumbling with the door latch.

She jumped up, searching her daughter's face for clues. "Well, did you get her? Or did you get her voice mail to leave a message?"

"I actually got her. She's at the police station waiting for Dad and the arresting officers."

"Arresting? So they're actually arresting him? Why? It's still his word against theirs."

"Maybe, but there are four of them, and it was his lighter they found, and it was Dad who had the argument with her." Mandy paused for a breath.

"Is there more?" asked Abby dreading the answer.

"Yes. Now the family is saying Dad was seen in the hallway going past the treatment rooms that night."

"Seen by whom?" asked Abby, already guessing the reply. "One of them?"

"I guess so."

"So that's how they're keeping themselves out of it. By dropping Richard right into it. Did the lawyer say anything else?"

Mandy gave her a look that slid away from her face as quickly as it landed. "She said to give you a message from her."

"What message?"

"Her exact words were, 'Thank Abby for sticking her nose in. Do me a favor and tell her to go back to Manitoba.'"

Mandy refused to make eye contact, and Abby wondered how much of the message she secretly agreed with. "She's right. It's my fault. I never should have stirred things up. I never should have come."

"I never should have asked you to cancel your plans," said Mandy. "I'm sorry, Mom."

They sat in silence for a few minutes, lost in their own thoughts and feelings. Mandy's stomach gave a loud gurgle and Abby said, "Lunch! We both missed it, and it's dinner time already. You must be starved. We better go down and have something."

"I don't think I could eat anything, Mom. You go."

"It's your stomach that's growling for food, so we'll both go. We're no good to anyone if we're weak from hunger. Come on. I don't feel like eating either, but look on it as a chore that has to be done, not a pleasure." Abby needed to talk to Mandy about her arranged rendezvous that night with Sylvia and Belinda, but she'd wait till she had some nourishment in her.

It had darkened totally by the time they entered the dining room. The lights reflected their images back at them in the large glass windows. Mona, Belinda, Jessie and Sylvia were sitting at a corner table. Abby and Mandy sat as far away from them as possible. By the looks of the table, they were already finishing their meal so would soon be gone. In any case, she had no intention of having any further conversations with Mona.

They ordered salads—a chicken Caesar for Abby and an Oriental chicken for Mandy. Both picked at their food, eating little.

Abby set down her fork. "I saw Sylvia in the parking lot when I went for a walk."

"And?"

"She was sort of apologizing for the family going to the police with their new story."

"What was new about it this time? It must have been a doozie of an interview for them to arrest Dad. So what new lies did they have to offer?"

"Sylvia only got started before she bolted away. She kept looking up at the windows as if afraid someone would see her talking to me, but she did admit actually seeing Kelly that night, not just arranging the meeting. She admitted talking to her."

"I don't understand. If she admits to lying and to seeing Kelly, how did that turn them against Dad?"

"I'm not sure. She still says the family didn't know about Kelly till afterwards, but there's lots she's not saying .She wants to though. Tonight."

Mandy gave a quick glance across the room to the table where the family seemed to be preparing to leave. "Is she coming to see us tonight?" She pushed her plate away and took a sip of coffee. "I don't see what good it will do to talk to any of them. We can't believe a word they say, and they're not exactly on our side."

Abby was disappointed. "I thought you'd be more pleased. If Sylvia wants to talk to me, it shows she may be willing to go against her family. We might find out something new."

Mandy looked up, her expression questioning, "You said 'me.'"

"She said she wants to talk to me alone. I think she feels

like you might be uncomfortable hearing what she has to say."

"How nice," said Mandy. "She's worried about my feelings."

"Don't be sarcastic. I don't think Sylvia has anything to do with Kelly's death. Maybe she thinks Richard doesn't either. So, in a way, she is on our side."

"Sh. They're headed this way."

The four women trouped past Abby and Mandy's table on the way out. Mona slowed for a moment, as though she was going to speak, but then she gave a smile, more of a satisfied smirk, and walked on. The other three trailed in her wake.

"I'm beginning to hate that woman," said Mandy.

"Me too. Do you get the feeling she's enjoying this?"

"Would she enjoy it so much if she were the one to kill Kelly? Or, would she just want to keep a low profile?"

Abby considered. "I don't think Mona ever keeps a low profile. She's more of a frontal attack person. That's one reason I don't think she's the one who killed Kelly."

"Why not? According to the police, Kelly was hit first and then moved. She drowned in that whirlpool. So, if she hit her in a fit of rage, the rest was covering up."

"I think, if Mona did it, she would have picked a place away from the spa somehow and would have finished her off at the start. She's too cool and collected than to leave it so she had to clean up after herself. No, I think Mona is in protective mode, so either one of the family did it, or she thinks they did. I wonder how much information the family actually shares with the others."

Mandy put her cup down, wiped her lips with her napkin, and folded it up in a roll under her plate. "Well, I've had enough for tonight. I'm going to try to sleep and then see if I can go talk to Dad in the morning. I hope they'll let me see him."

"I wouldn't count on it. Phone his lawyer first and arrange it through her."

Then Abby clattered her cup down in the saucer and stood up. "I'm coming up, too," said Abby. "I'll have a quick bath and wait for ten o'clock to go see Sylvia."

"Why not go now?"

"She wants to wait till Mona thinks she's in bed so we

won't be interrupted. Belinda is going to be there, too."

"Maybe she'll read your leaves while you're there." Mandy smiled for a brief second, but even the thought of her mother having her tea leaves read couldn't keep it there. Her mask of doom descended again.

"You don't sound happy about my talking to them."

"I just don't think it will do a lot of good. They've decided on the family line and will feed you what they want you to know." Mandy stopped suddenly on the stairs. "Say, did you ever think maybe this whole thing is Mona's idea in the first place, and she told Sylvia to make it look cloak and dagger to get your attention, so you'll believe everything they tell you?"

"When did you get so cynical?"

"I think it was when they arrested my father for murder." She turned quickly but not before Abby saw the tears glistening in her eyes.

Chapter Eighteen

The evening passed slowly. Mandy thumbed through some magazines she had picked up earlier in the gift shop, but Abby noticed her eyes weren't even making contact with the pages. She looked off at the painting on the opposite wall of an idyllic mountain glade. Abby was pretty sure it wasn't any interest in the mediocre artwork that held her attention.

Abby fumbled for the remote on the side table and turned on the television. Mandy's eyes flickered briefly to the screen and returned to their steadfast gaze at the snow-topped mountain. Abby thumbed through the channels but didn't find anything compelling enough to hold her interest. She left the television humming away on low volume just to cut through the thick miasma of depression that filled the room and said, "I'm going to take a bath. It's still a couple of hours till I can go to see Sylvia."

Mandy looked up at her. "Want a magazine?"

"No thanks. I have an old book I'll take in with me. Why don't you go to bed early?"

"I'm not tired." She flipped another page of her magazine.

Abby ran the water as hot as she could stand it and threw in some mango-scented salts. She stepped in, letting her body gradually become accustomed to the hot water and then leaned back in the tub, first splashing water on the slanted back to warm it.

She wondered what Richard was doing now. Was he sitting in a cell alone, or going over strategies with his lawyer, or being questioned by the police? Would they release him on bail so close to Christmas? Tomorrow was Christmas Eve. She arched her back and repositioned in the tub, trying to get comfortable. It was no use. The porcelain dug into her bones, and her tense muscles wouldn't unknot. She picked up the book she had brought in with her. A glance at the back cover blurb made her drop it back on the floor. A suspense story of a woman running from her possibly mad husband was not the sort of reading to calm her. Abby gave up. She might as well go sit in mutual despair with her daughter. She towelled off and rubbed some matching mango lotion into her damp skin.

Mandy looked up quickly from her magazine, still probably on the same page as when Abby had gone in. "That was quick," she said.

"I hate waiting for things," said Abby by way of explanation. "I wish ten o'clock would get here so I can find out what Sylvia and Belinda have to say for themselves." She took the towel back into the bathroom and draped it over the rod, giving the tub a quick wipe out with a used washcloth. Back in the living room, she said, "Why don't you take a bath? It will relax you more than those decorating magazines are doing."

"I'll wait till you get back," said Mandy.

They filled the rest of the evening with stand-up routines on a comedy network. None of the comedians sounded particularly funny, but it was a way to pass the time and occupy the darker recesses of the mind. She wondered what sort of life Sylvia had had all those years with the controlling Edward. She couldn't understand why she would stay. Then she thought of her own marriage and the times she'd nearly left Richard but had stayed. Her mind segued off to Edward's death. She wondered about the details. Twice now, she had heard an allusion to a horrible death. But then, what connection could that have to the present situation? She needed to keep focused on the important things.

At ten minutes to ten, Abby grabbed her purse and her room key. "Just in case I'm back late and you're asleep." She paused in the doorway. "Wish me luck."

"Luck," said Mandy with a forced smile. She obviously wasn't expecting anything good to come out of the evening.

She took the stairs to the third floor. The stairway and hallway were deserted except for a couple having a close snuggle beside the ice machine. She wondered why the subterfuge when they presumably had hotel rooms. At the end of the hallway, she pushed open the heavy glass door to the staff apartments.

This hallway, too, appeared deserted, but a flicker of movement down a side passage dispelled that thought. She glanced down the hall as she walked past and saw Theo, standing close to a young, dark-haired girl. She wondered if that was Stephanie, the manicurist. She'd have to ask Mandy what she looked like. From the brief glance she'd gotten of the couple, it hadn't seemed like a passionate embrace. Rather, Abby thought Stephanie had been handing Theo a small package. She thought again of the possibility of illicit drugs, but it seemed far-fetched. They would be a little more discreet if that were the case. Who knows? Maybe she was handing him a bag of jelly doughnuts.

She made a note to ask Mandy to check a little more into Stephanie's relationship with Theo. Or, maybe she should do it herself. It was a little early for Mandy to go for another manicure. Abby, on the other hand, needed one. She clutched her broken and unvarnished nails tighter at the thought. It would give her a chance to watch Stephanie's expression when she mentioned seeing the clandestine meeting. She still couldn't imagine anything between her and Theo being terrible enough to warrant killing Kelly. After all, they seemed to have no qualms about meeting in public, well, not so public hallways. They didn't seem upset that she had seen them. Maybe checking more into Theo and Stephanie was a waste of time.

She slowed at Sylva's door just as it opened, and she jumped back in surprise. Sylvia put her finger to her lips in a shushing motion and slid quietly into the hall, followed closely by the little white dog, closing the door behind her. She beckoned to Abby to follow and led her back the way she'd come, past the now deserted hallway where she'd seen Stephanie and Theo.

Sylvia stopped in front of another door marked S314 and knocked ever so softly. It opened immediately, and she, Sylvia, and the dog were ushered into the room by a kimono-clad Belinda.

No one spoke until they were all inside, and the door was closed and locked.

Abby looked at them inquiringly.

"Sorry for the fifth column tactics," said Belinda, "but this room is farther away from Mona's, and she is less likely to check on me than Mother, so we thought it would work better if we met here."

She motioned to a round table that sat in the dining nook, surrounded by four sturdy chairs upholstered in a plaid fabric. Abby sat down where she was bid. Sylvia sat across from her, the dog close at her side, and Belinda took the chair nearest the kitchen. "Sorry I had to bring Isis," she said. "If I'd left her alone she might have barked and Mona would hear her."

"I don't understand all the secrecy," Abby said. "If you're going to tell me something that will help Richard, I'm not exactly going to keep quiet about it." She bit her lip. That had probably not been the wisest thing to say to encourage confidences.

"We know that," said Sylvia. "We know you'll tell his lawyer anything that will help." She paused. "I'm not sure how to explain this to you."

"I am," said Belinda. "Look, we're not happy about what we told the police."

"You mean you told them a made-up story."

"Not exactly," said Belinda. "Well, maybe we fudged a little."

She turned away so that Abby couldn't read her expression and brought a tray over from the kitchen counter with three large mugs and a stainless coffee decanter. She began to pour before Abby could decline. They each took a mug, and Belinda removed the tray before speaking again.

"It's a little difficult to explain the family dynamics," she said. "You'd have to have known us to understand."

"So try to explain what I don't understand."

"We've always been a close family," Belinda began. "Not necessarily always close in affection, but in our ties to each other. Father was a bit of a tyrant." She sent an apologetic glance to her mother. "We learned to toe the line and do exactly what was expected of us. We discovered it was the only way to function, really."

"Mona changed," said Sylvia. "Somehow, she learned to

do what we couldn't do. She learned how to stand up to Edward and get away with it."

Belinda took over. "We never realized how alike Mona and Father had become until Father died." Belinda leaned forward in her chair. "She took Father's role in the family. We fell back into the old patterns after a while, just with a new head of family."

"But yet, you contacted Kelly," Abby directed her question to Sylvia. "That was going against your husband's wishes."

"Yes, I still can't believe I did it," said Sylvia. "That's why I made it all so cloak and dagger. I didn't want anyone to know until I had actually seen her. That way, if it didn't work out, I could pretend it never happened. And if it did, well, at least I had Belinda and Jessie here for support when I told Mona." She reached out and clasped her daughter's hand, giving it an affectionate shake before releasing it again.

"Jessie is a close part of your family group?" asked Abby.

"Oh yes," said Sylvia. "She's like a granddaughter to me. She used to spend her summers with us, and she made everything so much better just by being there. We should have asked her to come tonight, too." She looked at her daughter.

Belinda shook her head. "Best this way," she said.

"So how did Jessie get along with your husband?" Abby asked Sylvia.

"The same as the rest of us. I must have an innate character flaw," she said. "I seem to have picked a man just like my brother to marry. Arthur always dominated my life until I married. Then Edward took over the job."

Abby thought she must have rebelled a little against her family or there would be no Kelly to talk about.

"So what did you tell the police?" asked Abby, thinking they could be here till two o'clock discussing family relationships if someone didn't get to the point.

"Well," began Sylvia, glancing at Belinda as though for encouragement. "We told them the truth for the most part."

"It's the other part I'm most concerned about."

"We just embellished one little part," said Belinda, jumping in when Sylvia seemed not to know how to go on. "Maybe if we simply tell you what actually happened that night, we'll get to the other part afterwards."

"Fine with me," said Abby. Anything to get the show on the road.

They exchanged looks again. In some sort of silent agreement, Sylvia took the floor. "I was so excited about meeting Melody, well, I better call her Kelly. I had dreamed about it for years, all the time I was married to Edward. Then, when I finally got my chance and she agreed to meet me here, I was in heaven." Her eyes misted over, and she pulled a tissue from her robe pocket. She gave a quick blow and went on. "We arranged to meet after everyone would be in bed."

"How did you contact her?"

"I waited for Richard to leave the room. Kelly mentioned he smoked, so I knew he'd be going outside. When I saw him leave, I called the room and we made our arrangements."

"And they were?"

"We wanted to wait until everyone was in their rooms after dinner, and the cleaners had finished with the spa area. Kelly said she'd make up an argument with Richard to give her an excuse to leave the room without him."

"So even their argument was a fake?"

"Not really. Kelly said it started out as a ruse on her part, but they had been upset with each other before that, and it escalated into a real one. She said Richard was angry at her secrecy, and she just wanted him to leave her alone for a while without asking questions. She intended to tell him everything after we'd met."

Sylvia dabbed her eyes with a fresh tissue from a box Belinda had produced and snuggled her dog protectively on her knee. "We arranged to meet at the little anteroom because it was small and quiet, and we could slip in without anyone seeing us. The door from the corridor opens with a room key because of the gym upstairs, but the anteroom is kept locked. I made sure to get there first so I could unlock it."

Abby interrupted, "Did you see anyone else hanging around in the hallways?"

"No, if I had seen anyone, I would have gone back to my room and tried later. Anyhow, I wasn't there long when I heard a knock on the door. I rushed over to open it, and there she was."

Belinda patted her mother's tissue-filled hand comfortingly and silently.

Sylvia went on. "I can't describe to you how I felt at that moment, so I won't even try. Anyhow, we began to talk, and I tried to tell her how sorry I was for not contacting her before. She told me all about her childhood, her brute of a father, and the things he had done to her. She got more and more upset as she told me what her life had been like. She started to pace the room, and she was talking louder and louder. I was afraid someone would hear us. I put out my hand on her arm and asked her to lower her voice. She freaked out and shoved my hand away. When she did, she knocked over one of the jars of gel on the counter. It fell on the floor and broke."

"And," prompted Abby when she seemed stuck on that picture.

"I stooped down to pick up the mess and Kelly said 'Oh, for Pete's sake' and pushed me aside, saying she'd do it. Anyhow, she was wearing shoes with little spike heels on them and when she pushed me aside and rushed in, she slipped on the gel and fell. There's a gas fireplace in the room with a marble mantle. She fell into the fireplace and hit her head on the corner. Then she just lay there." Sylvia twisted her hands, shredding the tissue she held. Abby didn't want to break the silence. Sylvia gave a little gulp and repeated, "She just lay there. I could see the blood from where she'd hit the corner. She moved so fast and fell so hard. I couldn't see her breathing. I thought she was dead."

But she hadn't been dead. She'd drowned later in the whirlpool room. "So why didn't you call for help?"

"I did. I called Mona."

"I meant emergency services."

"I was so scared and so upset. I just didn't think. I ran to get Mona. She always knows what to do. She was upstairs in her suite. I couldn't think of any way to tell her what happened. I started to cry and told her she had to come with me. Mona being Mona, she wouldn't come without a reason, so I had to tell her about the meeting and about Kelly, a shortened version just to get her to come with me. Finally, she said she'd come along and check, but I knew she was thinking I was just babbling. Belinda was coming out of her suite as we passed. She came, too."

"How long was it between the time you left Kelly on the floor,"—Sylvia winced, screwing up her face as though about to cry, but gulped in a big breath of air instead—"and the time you went back downstairs?"

"Probably about fifteen minutes. It took a while for me to convince Mona to come. Then she had to get dressed. She was in her nightgown. And then we had to stop when Belinda came out."

"So fifteen minutes for someone to find out what happened, drag Kelly down the steps to the whirlpool, undress her, and drown her. For someone to kill her in that time, that someone had to be right there the moment you left. You're sure you didn't see anyone watching?"

"No, but I wasn't paying any attention. There could have been a parade of baboons for all I knew. I thought I had just killed my daughter!"

"Why did you think you had killed her? If she slipped, it was an accident. You wouldn't have been blamed."

"It wouldn't look that way. After not acknowledging her and meeting her in secret, it would have looked as though I was trying to keep her quiet, trying to keep her out of my life."

"Are those your thoughts, or what Mona told you to make you be silent?"

"Both, I guess. I was feeling guilty. I did think it was my fault she was dead. If only I'd stopped to be sure."

"With all this commotion, didn't anyone else come to see what was going on?"

"It wasn't really any commotion. In spite of being scared and upset, I was as quiet as I could be, and no one talked on the way down. I just wanted to show them what happened."

"So you saw no one in the hallways? No one at all?"

Another look at her daughter. "Well, on our way downstairs, we were looking around to be sure we weren't seen, so I know there was no one there. Until we got downstairs."

"And you saw someone then?"

"Just Jessie, but she saw someone. She was just coming out of reception. She'd left her purse in the office. She came along with us. Later, she said she saw a man going outside through the back door just before we arrived but never thought to mention it at the time. We got to the anteroom, and when we opened the door," Sylvia paused dramatically, "there was no one there. She was gone!"

"At first, Mona accused me of making it up or having a

bad dream or just being gaga. But then she noticed the blood on the mantle and the broken jar on the floor. There wasn't much blood. We cleaned it up, the gel, too, of course. Mona said it must not have been as bad as I'd thought, that I had exaggerated things as usual, and the best thing was to wait and see what she said in the morning."

"So you left it at that?" Abby's voice rose in incredulity.

"No, I had to go upstairs and tell the family all about it, the full story about Kelly and how I had given her up and how they had a half-sister."

"And this was news to them?"

Belinda broke in here. "It's exactly as Mother just said. None of us had any idea about who Kelly was."

"So what happened in the morning?"

"That part of the story is exactly the way we told everyone before."

"Tell me again," said Abby.

Another tissue, another nose clearing. The little dog stirred, circled in Sylvia's lap, gave her a quick lick on the chin, and settled down again. "I didn't sleep a wink. I don't know about anyone else. First thing in the morning, I tried to make myself believe I had a bad dream. It couldn't be true. But I knew it was. I knocked on Belinda's door, and we came downstairs together. Mona was already down. She was in the office, acting as though nothing had happened. By then, I thought maybe she was right. Maybe Kelly was just stunned, and maybe she got up and walked away with a sore head. I knew she'd be mad at me, but I even peeked in to the dining room to see if she was there."

"Why did no one do a check of the spa area the night before? If Kelly was stunned and walked away, didn't you think she could be concussed and confused and might be wandering somewhere, needing medical help?"

"No. We thought she'd just go to her room. Mona looked down the hall and didn't see anything."

Abby stopped herself from snorting in disbelief. She didn't want to alienate them and stop the flow of words. Sylvia and Belinda seemed to regard this as a sort of catharsis, that by telling someone outside the family they were absolving themselves of complicity.

"When did you decide something serious had happened to her?"

"We went into the dining room to have breakfast. We wanted to seem as normal as possible. Then your ex-husband—"

"Richard," Abby said. The family was reluctant to call him by name. They didn't want to feel close to someone they were framing for murder.

"Richard," Sylvia echoed. "He came down, looking as frazzled as I felt, and he started to question Jessie. Mona slipped out to reception to see what he had to say. He asked Jessie if anyone had seen Kelly. She said we hadn't, and he said she hadn't come back to the room last night. He said he was going to look around the spa area to see if she had gotten locked in a room somehow."

"But it was Jessie who went looking."

"Yes, she told him to wait here. She had all the keys to the storage rooms and could check better than he could. Belinda and I wandered out to the desk area, too. It was quiet. A few people were having breakfast, but no one was in the spa yet. The exercise room with the treadmills and weights is open first thing, but it's off by itself on the second floor. There might have been someone in there. Some early birds like to exercise before breakfast. But anyhow, Jessie went off and the rest of us waited. Theo came down the stairs and asked what was going on. We told him about Kelly disappearing. Then Jessie came running back, saying to call the doctor. Kelly was in the whirlpool, and she was dead."

"How did everyone react to that?"

"Mona told Jessie to call nine-one-one because she was the one who knew what she had seen. Richard," she said, calling him by name now, "immediately tried to run to Kelly. Mona told Theo to stop him and keep him here. He was resisting, saying maybe she was alive and hurt and needed him, but Mona got Theo to take him into the office and keep him there." She gave a little hiccup and stopped to take a swig of the now cold coffee.

Belinda took over the story. "Everybody was starting to raise their voices, and it was a bit of a ruckus, so I think Mona tried to keep a lid on things so as not to worry the other guests. There's not much more to it. Mona and Jessie sat in the office with Richard with the door closed. Mom and I went into the dining room. Now that we had Richard sort of cornered, Mona told Theo to go stand guard at the whirlpool and put up the closed sign to make sure no one else went to touch things. She said nothing should be disturbed."

"Nothing disturbed!" said Abby incredulously. "The original fall area had been cleaned up, Jessie had been down there, then Theo. Anyone could have stumbled down there during the night, and *now* she's worried about disturbing things?"

"You have to understand where Mona was coming from."

"Oh yes," said Abby with a touch of bitterness, "anything to protect the family name. It doesn't matter about anyone else."

They were all silent for a moment. Then Abby asked, "The man Jessie saw going through the back door. Did she get a good look at him?"

"Not really," said Sylvia, looking at Belinda as though for confirmation. "She said she didn't pay much attention at the time. She didn't realize it was significant until later. She just thought someone was going outside for a late night smoke."

"So when did she decide it was Richard she saw?"

Again, the exchanged glances. This time it was Belinda who answered. "She and Mona talked about it after the little confrontation the two of you had. We weren't invited to that conversation. I guess Mona convinced Jessie it was Richard and decided if we had to come clean about what happened in the anteroom, then we had to make sure there was somewhere to shift the blame."

"So you all picked on Richard."

"It was all decided before we went out. Jesse was the one to tell them. We were just along for moral support."

More like immoral support, thought Abby, but wisely only to herself.

"It all seemed to fit," said Sylvia. "After all, Richard and Kelly had had a fight, and he did smoke, and his lighter was found by the whirlpool. Who else could it have been?"

"But you didn't give the police a chance to come to their own conclusions. You presented them with a ready-made fact. Only, it wasn't a fact."

"That's why we decided to come to you," said Sylvia. Her expression took on a pleading look. "We didn't want to accuse Richard if he hadn't done it. We really thought he probably had. After we got back from the police station, Belinda and I met here and talked it over. We realized Mona had pushed us into saying things we only half-believed and thought you should know."

"You do realize that I am going to tell Richard's lawyer all of this? I'm not just going to accept your apology and sit on the information."

They both nodded. "We know. We'll have to face the music with Mona, and that's going to be difficult, but we'll do it together. It's time we both learned to stand up for ourselves."

"I'm so sorry." Sylvia took Abby's hand in her damp, tissue-holding one, and Abby had to refrain from pulling hers back. "We just couldn't accept the way we handled things. After all, if this goes to trial, we would have to go on the stand and swear to what we knew on oath. I don't think either of us could do that, so it's better to take our licks now."

"Who do you think really killed Kelly?" asked Abby, reclaiming her hand.

"Oh, Richard," they both said.

"You still think he did it?"

"Who else would want to? That's what the police think. It's what they thought before we told them about Jessie seeing him in the back hallway."

Abby sighed. It was going to be an uphill battle convincing everyone otherwise. Even the people who had lied believed him guilty. Well, she'd pass this on to Richard's lawyer and leave it to her to sway their opinions.

Chapter Nineteen

Abby was rising to leave when Belinda grabbed the three cups filled with now cold coffee and poured them out, refilling them from the carafe. "Stay just a moment longer," she said.

"Well, I did have another question for you. It's about access. You said there's another entrance to this section?"

"Yes, at the end of the hallway, right beside Mona's entrance. But, if you're thinking Mona could have slipped in there after doing away with Kelly, it's not possible. First, Mona may have her faults, but she's my sister, and I know she's not capable of violence. Secondly, Mother came right upstairs after Kelly fell and straight to Mona's room. She was there. No way was there enough time for her to move Kelly, drown her, and run up the stairs while Mother was coming up."

"That's not exactly what I was thinking," said Abby. "But thanks anyhow. I don't think Mona did it." She thought, *I'd love to think Mona did it, but it was, as they said, impossible.*

Abby didn't really want more coffee. She wasn't going to be able to sleep as it was. But she felt compelled to take a few sips of the brew.

Sylvia stood. Abby did, too. Sylvia motioned her back down and said, "I think Belinda wants to talk to you alone." She called to her little dog and left.

Abby looked at Belinda inquiringly.

"I know you don't believe in psychics or any of the things

I do," she began, "but I wanted to tell you about something I saw when Kelly and Richard arrived."

"What?" asked Abby, thinking, *This should be good.* She set her coffee down and slumped in her chair, trying to find a comfortable spot.

"I can see auras around people that tell me a lot about them." Belinda looked at Abby's skeptical expression and smiled. "All right. I know you're one of those people who don't believe in anything they can't feel or see, and I must admit I do add a little interpretation to my readings, which isn't difficult. People so want you to come up with certain scenarios, they practically give you a road map." She stopped and realized she had gone off track. "But the aura part is real. People do give off a sort of glow around them, and I can see it. You can tell a lot about people by their auras."

"I've heard of them, but what exactly are they? A sort of halo? Why would you see what no one else does? Is there any proof they exist?" Abby figured she might as well play along. Maybe Belinda had actually seen something, and she was using the aura as a way of telling her something without telling her.

Belinda didn't appear offended. She continued to smile. "I know you might find it difficult to understand, but yes, auras do exist. Not everyone can see them. I can, well, sometimes. Maybe everyone could if they just tried harder. It's not a sure thing. But I did see an aura around Kelly the night she arrived."

"You were downstairs when they checked in?" Abby thought she remembered an earlier conversation where Belinda denied seeing them. You never knew what to believe with this lot.

"Yes, Jessie had an emergency—you know a woman thing—and called me to cover for her while she went to change. I was the one who checked them in."

"This aura, you saw, was it just over Kelly or Richard as well?"

"It was mostly Kelly, but Richard had one, too. I told you. They aren't visible all the time. I only see them once in a while and usually when something significant is going on with the person involved."

Abby had no belief whatsoever in auras or any of the other mumbo-jumbo she imagined Belinda tried to push on her clients, but she saw no point in alienating her so she asked, "What did this aura look like?"

"I could tell right away she was hiding something. Her aura was a sort of murky blue and faded into a muddy brown."

"And what does that mean?"

"It means she was fearful about something she was planning to do. She was afraid of the future, afraid something bad was going to happen. But she was also secretive, hiding the truth."

Abby thought that was an easy thing to pin on an aura for a person that had been killed shortly afterward, while setting up a covert operation.

Belinda seemed to know what she was thinking. "You think I'm interpreting in retrospect, but I'm not. I promise you, Kelly was in a confused state of mind that night."

"I don't see how that helps us, even if I do grant you the ability to see these auras. It doesn't say anything new."

"Oh, but it does. I never told you about the aura around Richard's head."

Abby jerked her head up. She didn't believe in this. She really didn't. But she was captivated by the idea of knowing the unknown. "And what did you see around Richard?" she asked as casually as she could.

"It was orange."

"And what does that mean?"

"It means, or could mean, a lot of things. Looking back—"

"Don't look back. That's just you guessing. What did you think at the time?"

"I thought they were a mismatched pair. She was so secretive, he so open. An orange aura means he gets along well with everyone, wants people to like him. He doesn't understand secrecy and aloneness, and she was giving off waves of everything he shouldn't like. But there's another side to orange as well. Orange could mean a temper, an act now and think later sort of person. That's the part that made me understand he could be the type to hurt someone in anger if the circumstances were right."

Abby tried to reconcile the description with her version of Richard. Her mind stuck on the "open" reference. Richard might appear open most of the time, but Abby knew he was certainly capable of keeping secrets, too. He had done so in their marriage, and done so well.

"I'm sorry. I don't believe a word of this, but even if I did, Kelly wasn't killed in anger. She was killed after her fall, not in a fit of rage. Someone moved her and drowned her. Does that still look orange to you?"

Belinda looked away as though in thought for a moment. "Maybe not. Maybe I was looking at it from the wrong direction. I'll have to see what shows the next time I see him."

Abby stood up. What a ridiculous way to end the evening. "I'd better get back. My daughter will be worried."

"Would you like to hear what sort of an aura you have?"

"No," said Abby shortly.

Belinda chuckled. "It's interesting. If you ever change your mind, let me know."

Chapter Twenty

Abby left the room and practically flew down the hall. She couldn't wait to tell Mandy about everything she had heard. In other circumstances, the last bit about the auras would have been an amusing story, leaving them in laughter, but not tonight. The important bits were encouraging as far as Richard was concerned.

When Abby opened the door, Mandy was pacing the floor and whirled to face her.

"Where have you been?" she demanded.

"You know where I was, with Sylvia and Belinda."

"All this time? I was getting worried. In case you've forgotten, we've had one murder here. I don't want you added to the list."

"Yes, Mother," said Abby in feigned meekness.

"Sorry," said Mandy with a ghost of a smile. "I was getting nervous. You were gone so long. Was it worth it?"

"I think so. Let me tell you everything, and we can figure out exactly how to put it when we call Richard's lawyer in the morning." Abby glanced at the clock to confirm the time. "Eleven-thirty. It's definitely too late to call anyone tonight."

Tired of coffee by now, Abby poured a glass of wine, knowing she'd regret it in the middle of the night. They sat down on the sides of the bed, facing each other as Abby recounted the details of the evening. She stopped once or twice to backtrack and insert something she'd missed the first go-round. When finished, she asked, "So what do you think?"

Mandy said, "At the very least, it's hopeful. As long as Belinda and Sylvia don't change their minds and deny what they said. At least it shows the first part of Kelly's death had nothing to do with Dad."

"And that's the important part. If the police thought Richard hit Kelly in anger and then moved her to finish the job, it sort of changes the whole motivation. Why would he move Kelly and drown her? The heat of the argument motive is out the window. And, if he had some other reason, why would he move her? Why not kill her there and make it look as though Sylvia was responsible?"

"I'll feel a lot better when we can tell Taylor Couling all about it."

"Couling?"

"The lawyer."

"Why can I never remember her name?"

"You never remember people's names. And you don't like her, so you doubly don't remember hers."

"You're right. I don't like her, but it doesn't matter how I feel if she can get the job done, and she does look very capable."

It was nearly two o'clock by the time they turned the lights out. Strangely, Abby fell asleep right away, a dreamless sleep that remained undisturbed until she woke with a pressing need for the bathroom. Grumbling about coffee and aging bladders, she peered at the clock as she swung her legs over the edge of the bed. Seven thirty, nearly time to get up. She decided, as long as she was in the bathroom, she might as well have her morning shower and free it up for Mandy when she got up.

By the time she came out of the shower, towel wrapped around her head and rubbed down with lotion under her robe, Mandy was up and waiting for her turn.

Abby put the coffee packet in the brewer and waited impatiently for it to come down. She pulled on her clothes and poured a cup of coffee as soon as it was ready. She knew it was much too soon to call Couling—*there, she remembered her name!*—but was anxious to get it over with. She knew there probably wouldn't be too much warmth in her reception. She would be reminded she had been told to keep out of it. Well, she hadn't exactly pushed herself in. Belinda and Sylvia had commandeered her.

Mandy rummaged through the dresser drawers. It didn't matter how many clothes she'd brought, she'd never find the one she wanted until she had searched through all of her options. She gave a little gasp and slammed the drawer shut.

"What is it?" asked Abby, alarmed.

Mandy slumped down beside her on the bed. "I almost forgot about Christmas after everything that's happened. It's Christmas Eve today. I just opened the drawer, and there were the gifts I'd brought for Dad and Kelly. Now, Dad is in jail, and I'll never see Kelly again."

Her voice rose on the last part of the sentence, and Abby threw her arm over her daughter's shoulder, pulling her close. "It's all right, love. Your dad will be home soon, and then we'll have our own Christmas to celebrate this all being over." She couldn't think of a thing to say about Kelly's present. She considered slipping it out of the drawer and hiding it away somewhere.

By the time they were dressed and had finished the coffee, Abby thought it was late enough to contact the lawyer. She connected with Ms. Couling while Mandy brushed her teeth and did her hair. She wanted privacy to make the call. She wasn't saying anything she wouldn't tell Mandy later, but it was a call she felt nervous and awkward making. She managed to explain, without getting too tongue-tied, what Belinda and Sylvia had told her. She emphasised they were willing to stick with their new story if it ever came to court. The lawyer was distant but polite. Abby tried to ask if there was anything new, but the lawyer merely said things might not be as bad as they had looked. She even said thank you without the sarcastic note this time. Mandy came out of the bathroom at the end of the call, and Abby gave her the gist of the conversation.

They trooped down the stairs to breakfast in a much better frame of mind. If even the dour-faced attorney saw hope ahead, they would be doubly optimistic.

As they passed the desk, Abby glanced over to see which of the family would be out and about this morning. Jessie was there, back turned towards them, facing a tall, gaunt man Abby recognized as Arthur.

They were arguing. At least, Jessie was. Her voice was low enough Abby couldn't hear her words, but they were forceful and full of fury. She moved a little closer, wondering how far she could get without making her interest obvious. She browsed through a rack of brochures, straining to hear. She could only make out the odd word. "Sylvia...leave her alone...warning..." Grandfather Arthur didn't seem to be taking her too seriously. His smile became a smirk, and then he gave a short laugh and started to turn from her. Jessie raised her voice then. "I mean it," she said in a biting and bitter tone. "I won't let you hurt her. I won't let anyone hurt her." Andrew's eyes slid over Jessie's head and made contact with Abby's.

Jessie turned and shouted, "What do you want?"

Abby opened her mouth to find an excuse for loitering by the brochure rack, but Jessie gave her no time to formulate a reply. She whirled around and rushed into the office, the door closing with a bang behind her.

Arthur came out from behind the reception desk and said, "Ms. Addison, I believe?"

"Yes, and you're Jessie's grandfather?"

He didn't deign to answer the question, instead posing one of his own. "I find it difficult to understand, considering the circumstances of your visit, why you're still here at the spa, poking your nose around into things." His eyes were cold and his expression dismissing.

Instead of making her feel cowed, his supercilious attitude brought out a duelistic force in Abby. She snapped back, "We're staying here until my daughter's father is released from police custody, and the true killer is arrested. It would happen a lot more quickly if your family didn't continually feed the police false information." And with those parting words, Abby turned to flounce like the heroines she always admired in old movies. It was a trifle difficult to do the maneuver properly in jeans and tennis shoes, especially while trying to stuff brochures back in their slots in the rack.

Oh well, she may have failed at the gesture, but she was pretty sure she got her point across. She didn't turn to see if Arthur was laughing at her or staring in confusion.

She looked around for Mandy and saw her coming out of the salon. "Mission accomplished," Mandy told her. "Stephanie said if I popped in after lunch she'd fix my broken nail, no charge."

"Oh, terrific." After a few steps, Abby realized Mandy wasn't following her into the dining room and turned to see her standing still. "There's more," her daughter said with a teasing smile.

"What?" Abby retraced her steps and leaned close enough towards Mandy for a conspiratorial whisper.

"I managed to let her know that you saw her with Theo last night. It's a little difficult working something like that into a conversation, so I'm rather pleased with myself."

"What did she say?"

"You were almost right."

"Steroids? Drugs?"

"No. Muffins. Remember you said it could be a bag of doughnuts for all you knew? Well, not doughnuts, but muffins. Someone at some time must have told Stephanie the way to a man's heart is through his stomach, and she keeps bringing him little gifts. I don't think it's working though. She was talking about trying an old recipe of her grandmother's for rhubarb cobbler next."

"Somehow, I wouldn't think gifts containing sugar and all those other unhealthy ingredients would be the best choice for someone as body image conscious as Theo."

"That's what I thought, too. I even made a suggestion or two."

"And?"

"She changed her mind about the cobbler and is going to make an on-line search for a recipe for no sugar, low-fat zucchini loaf instead."

"Good for her." On that happy note, Abby and Mandy went in search of breakfast.

Chapter
Twenty-One

Abby was hungrier this morning than she had been for days. She was feeling quite optimistic after her chat with Ms. Couling. The hint that things might be about to improve for Richard sent her to the griddle section of the breakfast buffet. She filled a plate with scrambled eggs and bacon, toast with honey packs and then stopped for a glass of orange juice before grabbing her essential fix of coffee. When she got to their table, she was pleased to see Mandy was obviously rediscovering her appetite, too.

They ate without conversation, Abby's eyes wandering around the dining room. Not a busy time at the spa. Most people were headed home for their family dinners or waiting till after the holiday food orgies to worry about improving their bodies. A family of four sat by the large window—the same family Abby remembered seeing their first day here. They, too, sat in silence, but their stiff body postures and stilted movements suggested it was not the comfortable silence she and Mandy were sharing. Another day, Abby's curiosity about other people's lives might have sent her into a speculative frenzy of scenarios, but now she had enough in her own life to gnaw at. Two more tables held couples. One woman sitting alone, apparently lost in a book occupied sat at another table. Of course, the dining room had been open for an hour or more. Maybe the main crowd had come and gone.

A movement to her left brought her attention to the entrance. Mona paused in the doorway for a moment, her eyes scanning the room, sliding over Mandy and Abby as though they were of no importance. Now there, Abby thought, was someone with the ability to make a Hollywood entrance. She would have dealt with Andrew with panache and pizzazz. It was impossible not to look up. She crossed to the other side where she sat at what must have been her exclusive table. It was the only one Abby had seen her at. She was by herself. No Belinda, no Sylvia. Abby wondered if that was her choice or theirs. Were they avoiding her, not wanting to acknowledge their revelations of last night? Or, had Mona found out and sent them to Coventry?

Mandy set down her fork with a big sigh. Abby followed suit. "I'll probably regret this later," she said, "but that was the best breakfast I've had in ages."

"Me, too. When you talked to the lawyer," Mandy began, bringing them back to the world of real problems, "did she say why she felt more optimistic?"

"No, but she wouldn't tell me anything, would she?"

Another guest appeared in the doorway, pausing to look around the room before strolling over to join Mona at her table. It was Arthur, but there was no sign of his buddy Jack, also known as see no evil.

"Making an entrance seems to run in the family," murmured Abby.

"What?"

"Nothing. Just grumbling. I have to tell you about Arthur and Jessie, but I'll wait till we get to the room. Mona looks happy to see her uncle. She seems to be the only one." Jessie's match with him in the office seemed to confirm what Tillie had told them about him. Indeed, the objects of their gossip looked as though they were beginning a quite amicable conversation. Mona was actually smiling, and Arthur almost lifted his lip corners. It was probably something he did so rarely the muscles needed a work out before they would function properly, thought Abby.

"Ready to go?" she asked out loud.

In assent, Mandy picked up her purse and led the way to the stairs. As they passed the gift shop, Tillie gave them a merry wave and came to the front to waylay them.

"I imagine you're both relieved this morning," she said.

"It will make a better Christmas for you both."

"Sorry," said Abby. "I'm not sure what you mean."

"Oh, you haven't got the good news yet. Well, I won't tell you and spoil the surprise then."

With that, she turned and clicked back to the counter of her shop on her very high, very un-old-ladylike heels. Mandy and Abby looked at each other and shrugged. Then the same thought apparently coming to them both at the same time. They sprinted up the stairs. Mandy flung open the door to their room. It was empty. Grabbing another key from the desktop where she kept her father's spare, she rushed out the door and down the hall, taking the stairs to the third floor two at a time. Abby was close on her heels but managing only one stair at a time.

Chapter Twenty-Two

Mandy gave a quick knock before inserting her key into the lock on her father's room and swung the door open.

"Daddy!" she shouted and flung herself into his arms. "When did you get out? Have they dropped the charges? What's going on? Did they find out who really did it?"

Richard hugged his daughter fiercely, meeting Abby's eyes over her shoulder. He laughed, and it was music to Abby's ears.

"One question at a time." He sat down and patted the bed beside him. Mandy took her place beside him, and Abby drew a chair over so that she was facing them both.

"They didn't drop the charges." Two faces fell at that news. "So obviously they haven't found out yet who did it. But Taylor managed to pull in a few favors and got a quick bail hearing for me. I was able to put the house up for security, and here I am. I'm not out of the woods by a long shot, but Taylor said she had some new lines to investigate." He cast a look at Abby. "I think you had something to do with that. Anyhow, she's hopeful we can get it cleared up without going to trial."

"Now," he said, rubbing his hands together, "I think we should put the whole sad mess out of our thoughts for a day and think about Christmas. It's tomorrow in case you've forgotten."

Abby agreed but was a little disconcerted at the way he was able to brush off the death of the woman he loved and wanted to marry. She studied his face. The pouches under his eyes, the emphasized lines around them, and the hard set to his mouth told another story. He was putting on a brave face for his daughter.

"There's a midnight service at a little chapel ten miles or so down the road. I heard someone talking about it yesterday," said Mandy. "We could go to that."

Richard sent a questioning lift of his eyebrow to Abby.

"It sounds fine with me," she said. It was certainly a lot better than sitting around a hotel room. She had no interest in going downstairs to listen to pop versions of Christmas carols as they were served eggnog and fancy sandwiches promised in the events calendar. On second thought, maybe they could do both. It wouldn't hurt to stop in at the spa celebration on the way to church. Maybe they would pick up some snippets of conversation from the Davenports. No, they probably wouldn't even be there other than a brief hostess appearance from Mona. It was best to stick with plan A. They needed to forget the unpleasantness for one evening and try to be normal.

Richard's cell phone rang, and Abby and Mandy both jumped. It didn't take much to send their thoughts back to the murder. Richard looked at the screen. "David," he said. "I phoned him yesterday but got his answering service. I wanted to tell him everything before it hit the news." He put the phone to his ear and sent out a jolly hello.

A little late for that, thought Abby. Unless he's a hermit, his brother had likely already watched it on the news. She and Mandy started to get up at the same time, to leave Richard alone to talk.

Richard waved them back down again, holding up his cigarette pack with the other hand, signalling that he would go out for a smoke. They sat back down.

Abby hoped Matthew wouldn't get the news in his distant part of the world, but with the immediacy of social networking in even remote places she couldn't be sure. Unable to contact him, she had left a message with a coordinator in the group, telling him of her changed plans for Christmas, and there had been an accident, but the three of them were fine. She promised more details later and wished he'd call. Then she reached for her cell phone to check its charge and re-membered she'd left it on the dresser.

To Mandy, she said, "I'd better run back and get my phone in case your brother calls."

She sped through the hallway and took the stairs to the second floor. As she looked down the winding staircase to the first floor, she could see a familiar trio slowly ascending. She had no place to duck and hide so forced herself to slowly walk down the second floor hallway, away from the staircase, her back to Sylvia, Arthur and Jessie. They followed her, ap-parently not recognizing her from behind, or maybe just en-grossed in their own conversation. Why were they on the second floor? Both Jessie and Sylvia had suites on the third floor in the staff wing. Oh, but maybe Arthur didn't. He'd be in a guest room. She heard Sylvia's voice, low and tearful. She couldn't make out a single word. Arthur's response was controlled and quiet. She suspected he rarely needed to raise his voice to get results. Jessie's voice was a little louder and a little less controlled. "Aunt Sylvia did nothing wrong," she said. "I mean it, Grandfather."

She could almost sense them stopping then, knew from the prickles on her spine that they recognized the solitary walker in front of them.

"Good evening, Ms. Addison," said Arthur. "Out for a stroll or on reconnaissance?"

She turned to see a snarky smile and knew he was the source of the shiver she'd felt earlier. What a horrid man. How did his family put up with him? From all accounts, Ed-ward must have been similar in nature. At least no one had to put up with him anymore. Abby chided herself for another uncharitable thought. Again, she wondered just how Edward had died. Two people had referred to it as a horrible death. They also called it an accident. Car crash? Fall from a cliff? What other accident could be described as horrible? *Anything that killed you.*

"On my way to my room, thanks. And good evening to you, too." Abby was beside her own door now and shoved her key card in with a violent thrust, happy to be away from them. She would have liked to talk to Sylvia and Jessie, true, but not in the presence of Arthur. It would also have been impossible to talk to Sylvia in Jessie's presence. She had ob-viously assumed the role of protector to her great-aunt.

She checked her cell phone. No missed calls and no new messages or texts. She wasn't sure if that should make her relieved or worried. She was happy if Matthew hadn't heard all the news, but concerned that it meant he was in difficulty somewhere, not able to communicate.

Why did all the child-rearing books stop at the teen years? There were as many things to worry about when they grew up. *There should be a manual on how to cope with your adult children.*

Abby sighed and sat on the edge of the bed, her head bowed in discouragement. Her phone rang. She snatched it up. Matthew? No. the screen showed an unknown caller. But that could still be him.

"Hello," she said eagerly into the phone.

Chapter Twenty-Three

The answering voice was familiar but not the one she was expecting. A sense of disappointment flitted trough her, but she pushed it back down.

"Neil. How is the holiday going?"

"The sunshine is great, the sand is perfect, and the sea is a stunning blue. The only thing missing is your wonderful smile. Is there any chance you can make it before I have to leave?"

"It doesn't look like it," Abby said. "The good news is Richard managed a bail hearing and is here for Christmas. The bad news is, well, I guess the bad news is that there is no other news."

"So he gets to spend the holidays with two beautiful ladies in his life. Not a bad way to celebrate Christmas."

"I'm not one of the ladies in his life, Neil. In case you've forgotten, Kelly was, and she's dead."

"Sorry. My sense of tact goes out the window after three double rums. I miss you and just wanted to say hello."

Abby's indignation faded. "I miss you, too. You must be down at the pool. I hear music in the background."

"No such luck. Cell phones are a prohibitive rate from here. I'm using a phone by the bar closest to the beach."

"Tom and Traci with you?"

"No, they took a tour somewhere. I felt more like being a sloth today, so I'm on my own."

Abby wondered. She heard a woman's laugh nearby, soft and seductive. She wished she weren't so plagued with mistrust and self-consciousness when it came to her relationships with men. Thank Richard for that, she thought with a touch of bitterness. She had trusted Richard in every aspect of their lives. She still did in every way except the one that had counted in their marriage.

"Abby?"

"Sorry. Did I miss something? The connection must be spotty."

"No, I just had a feeling for a minute you were off in another world. Is Mandy with you?"

"No, I'm here alone. She's in Richard's room. We're trying to decide how we can make Christmas not as terrible as it seems to want to be."

"I wish I could help in some way. Maybe I should have followed you out there instead of joining Tom and Traci."

"Don't be silly. There's nothing you could do to help, even if you are a lawyer."

"Not my field anyway. I'm a whiz if you need a contract, but something like this, well... Try to let things go for the day and have a happy day with your daughter." Abby noticed he didn't include Richard this time. "I guess I'd better let you go. Maybe we can have a getaway later if our schedules will allow, after everything is sorted out. Say, you know what? Tomorrow at six o'clock have a Christmas drink, and we'll toast each other. I'll work out what time that would be here. Sound like a plan?"

Abby laughed. Her black mood had a chink of light coming in. "It's a deal. I'm glad you're the one to do the time conversion. I was never good at that."

"Salut then, until tomorrow."

"Until tomorrow."

She sat for a moment with the phone in her hand, picturing Neil as he turned away, throwing his head back with the gesture he always used to tame the lock of dirty blond hair that continually fell over his right eye. His lean form would be strolling now to the beach, hands in his shorts pockets, unless they were holding a couple of rum drinks. He would probably be whistling, something he did when he was pleased. She wished she were beside him, walking hand in hand, feeling the hot tropical sun instead of listening to the whisper of the cold snow swirling outside.

She sighed and rose, putting the cell along with her key in her jeans pocket.

Chapter Twenty-Four

When she got back upstairs to the room, Richard was back from his phone call and smoke break. Mandy was holding a small box. She looked up and smiled, tilting the box so Abby could see the tiny gold earrings that lay in a silver cloud. They were gold and the dangles were in the shape of puppies. "Aren't they pretty?" she asked.

Abby held the box closer to look. "Yes, and very appropriate considering your chosen line of work."

"I know I'm a day early," said Richard, "but I thought it might brighten the day. I have something for you, too, Abby."

"For me?" For one awful moment, she hoped he wasn't going to give her a gift originally intended for Kelly, but she pushed the thought down immediately. Of course, not. This was Richard.

"I picked it up in the gift shop on the way up." He handed her a little box like the one Mandy held. "That gift store lady is quite the talker, isn't she?"

"Oh, Tillie is definitely a one-off," agreed Abby, opening the box. "Also, a fountain of information." She made a mental note to ask Tillie when she had the chance about Edward's accident. She turned her attention back to the tiny box. Nestled inside was a little silver charm, a cat.

"I hope you still have that charm bracelet. I haven't seen you wear it here, but I know you had it at Matthew's party.

This charm reminded me of Ajax."

"Thank you," said Abby simply. She leaned over and gave him a quick hug. "Yes, I still have the bracelet. It's in the room."

She felt a prickle of tears and tried to shrug them off. Richard had always been able to do this to her. No matter what he had done or what problems they suffered in their marriage, he would make some sweet gesture, and all the bad thoughts would be wiped from her mind. What other man would remember a bracelet his ex-wife wore weeks ago? Or even remember the name of her cat? But then once upon a time, Ajax had been his cat, too.

"I don't have anything for you," she said to Richard. "And Mandy's gifts are at home. I left in such a hurry. We'll open them when all this is over."

"Your being here is all the gift I need," said Mandy. "Thanks for dropping everything when I called."

"I second that," said Richard, prompting a round of hugs. "What are our plans for the day?"

"The turkey dinner downstairs is at two, I think, and a self-serve lunch for the evening. We have a couple of hours to fill before turkey."

"Once I've had the turkey, I'm done for the day," said Richard. "Undo my belt, turn on some music and nap the serotonin away."

"I think we're all going to be snoozing this afternoon," said Mandy. "Why don't we go for a drive? There's nothing constructive we can be doing, so let's try to unwind a little."

"I'll drive," said Richard, picking up the keys from the bedside table. He must have received a sample of Mandy's heavy foot, too, thought Abby with a smile. Her smile disappeared quickly when she thought maybe it was her driving he was trying to avoid. She wasn't a bad driver, not a speeder, never careless, but Abby knew she was more easily distracted than most people.

They took the winding road out from the spa and followed the highway down the island. Not the functional, bland highway they had come in on, but the original Island Highway—a two lane road not designed for speed but picturesque scenes and guaranteed to induce a sense of calm and relaxation. They pulled off on a spot where they could park and watch the ocean and just sat there for a quiet interlude, enjoying the majesty of Mother Nature at her best.

"Anyone for ice cream?" asked Richard on the way back.

"It's winter!"

"Doesn't stop the ice cream from tasting good," he replied. "There's a little country store we passed on the way down that has a few flavors all winter long. Taylor mentioned it."

Taylor? When did she find time to be discussing ice cream when she was supposed to be solving a murder? Well, maybe not solving a murder, Abby corrected herself, but keeping Richard from being convicted of one.

"We had a long wait for the bail hearing, and she was telling me about the shop. Her daughter owns it. Ready to give it a try?"

He glanced sideways at Abby who was riding shotgun, but since he had already flicked his signal light on, there wasn't much point in answering.

Abby was glad they stopped. She ordered raspberry cheesecake, and it was creamy and delicious. Richard had Sasquatch Trails with bits of chocolate and nuts in it and Mandy had rocky road, her favorite. She wondered if the young girl with the long ponytail was Taylor's daughter. She couldn't make out a resemblance, but you could never tell which side of the gene pool a child would pull their looks from. She didn't ask and neither did Richard.

She looked at her watch when they got back in the car. Good thing they had only had single scoops. By the time they got back, it was nearly time for turkey dinner with all the fixings.

At the spa, the wonderful smell of turkey, dressing, pumpkin pie, and a whole medley of other mouth-watering aromas assailed them. People were standing around in the lobby area, small glasses of champagne in hand, compliments of the spa, waiting to be told dinner was ready. They weren't a large group but looked ready to enjoy themselves. A Christmas song came through the speakers with such assurance by the singers it was easy to believe in the possibility of joy in the world. Spa guests stood in small groups, the hum of conversation buzzing beneath the music. Everyone was dressed in their Sunday clothes. Soon, a chef in traditional garb appeared at the entrance to the dining room and clanged at a small but sweetly sounding triangle. With a flourish, he indicated they should follow him into the dining room. No one needed coaxing.

Abby couldn't see any sign of the Davenport family. She thought they might have made an appearance to wish the guests a Merry Christmas, and maybe they had just missed it. In all probability, they were having a family dinner in Mona's room. It made for a much more pleasant atmosphere, Abby thought, not having to avoid Mona's caustic glances.

Although the chef had made his grand entrance, the meal was attended by a minimum of staff. It was set up buffet-style, and there were two servers along with the chef who presided at the carving of the turkey. He made a quick retreat when the line had finished, probably off to his own home and family.

In spite of the ice cream appetizer, they all managed to clean their plates. Miraculously, they made it through the whole meal without once mentioning Kelly's death.

Instead, they talked about the past, reminiscing over some of the Christmases when Mandy and Matthew had been children.

"If we're having the big dinner today, what do we eat tomorrow?" asked Mandy. "It's only Christmas Eve, after all."

Abby smiled. "I think it will be just like home. Leftovers for the next two days. I imagine that's why they had the big deal today. Most of the staff will get Christmas off, except for an unlucky one or two that will get stuck making do."

"Do you ever feel sorry for the people who have to work holidays?" asked Mandy.

"Sometimes, but it's not all bad, working the holidays. I'm sure they split up the days off. I used to work in a hotel when I was in college, and I actually asked for the chance to work the big days. The extra pay was pretty inviting to a poor student. I still got my turkey dinner, maybe a day early or a day late. It's not quite so nice if you have young children and have to work around schedules when husbands and wives work shifts."

"Hmm. I don't think I'd like to work Christmas Day."

"Just wait, young lady. You won't be immune. Veterinarians may close their offices on Christmas, but someone has to be on call. I bet the newest grads are the ones that get stuck."

"Being on call isn't quite the same as putting in a full day after or before eating a big turkey dinner."

Two pieces of pie for Richard and one each for Abby and Mandy, and they were ready to call it quits. They even took the elevator up to their rooms.

When Abby and Mandy got out of the elevator on the second floor, Richard said, "I may just sleep till morning. Turkey always does that to me. If I don't come down before, wake me when it's time for the Christmas Eve service."

Abby said, "I'm going to take a stroll. I'll be back shortly." She didn't wait for protests from Mandy, but took the stairs back down to the lobby. There was a "closed" sign on the gift shop door, but she could see Tillie inside. She could be catching up on books or doing inventory. You'd think she'd be happy to be gone on Christmas Eve, but then Tillie probably led a lonely life.

She managed to make eye contact with Tillie and waved. Tillie came over to the door and swung it open. "I'm closed now," she said," but if there is something you need, I can get it for you."

"Oh no, not really. I'm just trying to wear off some of the dinner and kill time while the rest of the family take their naps." A bit of a lie, but she wanted to connect with Tillie so that she'd start a conversation. It worked. Tillie motioned her inside.

"I have some coffee on the go. Would you like some?" Then she grinned. "Or even better, I have a bottle of sherry in the back."

"That sounds perfect," said Abby.

Chapter
Twenty-Five

They settled in the dimly lit shop behind the desk in two not very comfortable chairs, and began small talk about the weather, the spa, and Christmas.

Once they had finished about half the sherry, Abby turned the conversation to Edward's accident.

"You mentioned, and I think Sylvia did, too, that Edward had some sort of horrible accident. How exactly did he die?" To anyone else it might seem an impertinent question, but Abby thought Tillie might not mind. She didn't.

She took another long sip of sherry. "He took a fall down the stairs."

"Oh, that would be horrible."

"That wasn't the horrible part. He was coming down from his office at the time with some letters he was opening. He had a letter opener in his hand. He tripped and fell down the flight of steps and landed on the letter opener."

Abby let out a long slow whistle. "And the letter opener was business side up?"

"Yep. The stairs were lethal. Sylvia had tripped on the carpet at the top and nearly took a spill a few weeks earlier. They were too steep, according to an inspector who looked at them afterwards and said they should have been repaired."

"The police ruled it an accident? Didn't it look suspicious to them? Did they question the family?" Abby was asking questions she knew she hadn't the right to ask, but she wondered if, in some strange way, Edward's death could be related to Kelly's, although she didn't see how.

"Yes, yes, and yes. I'm sure they wondered about the way he landed holding the letter opener that way, but they had a re-enactment of some sort and said it could have happened that way. The letter opener wasn't really a letter opener, at least not the kind you buy in a gift shop. It was an old dagger of some sort. It belonged to Sylvia, but they used it as an opener. They had no evidence to prove it wasn't an accident."

"Who was home at the time?"

"Just Sylvia." She took another sip of sherry, emptying the glass and set it down beside the bottle. "Oh, and I think Jessie had come to visit that day. Yes. I think she was the one who called the ambulance."

"Not the police?"

"Oh, they came, too. Edward was almost, but not quite dead when they arrived, so they had to get him in the ambulance right away. They didn't have time to take all those pictures like they do on TV. Just a quick snap or two and Edward was on his way to the hospital."

"So no evidence that it was anything but an accident?"

"I guess not. Oh, but one funny thing happened."

"Funny? What was that?"

"The letter opener went missing."

"How could it get lost?"

"I don't know. The policeman who questioned Sylvia and Jessie was upset about it. Asked them if they had seen it. They hadn't, of course. You wouldn't be paying attention to a letter opener when someone was dying at the foot of the stairs. I guess they thought it got lost in the ambulance when it went with the body, but they checked everywhere. Rather embarrassing for them, I guess."

"I imagine they were quite happy to rule it an accident. Imagine having to explain how they lost the murder weapon at the scene of the crime."

Tillie chuckled and pointed to the not quite empty bottle of sherry. "A tad more?" she asked.

"No, I'd better go see how my family is doing. And I imagine you want to get home for the big day tomorrow." It was difficult to tell in the dim light, but Abby thought Tillie's face clouded over at the mention of Christmas.

"Yes, I should go, too." She stood slowly and took the bottle and glasses to the back. "Thanks for the conversation."

"Thanks for the sherry." Abby stood for a moment and watched as Tillie puttered with tidying. She almost asked if she would like to come up and have Christmas Eve with them, maybe go to the special service with them. Then she thought better of it and turned to leave. She couldn't just invite someone without checking first with Mandy and Richard to see if they wanted to give up family alone time to share with a stranger. If things went wrong and Richard went to jail, it might be the last time they shared for quite a while. Then, too, Tillie might find the invitation condescending or an act of pity. And who knows, maybe she had someone waiting for her at home. It was silly to speculate about someone's home life when you didn't know squat about them.

Abby trudged up the stairs to the room. The hallways were empty. She heard music and laughter coming in little waves through the doors as she passed the row of rooms to her own. Christmas Eve held happiness for most of the people here. Maybe she, Mandy, and Richard could snatch a little of it for themselves.

She opened the door to the low hum of a television. Mandy was stretched out on the bed, sound asleep. Richard had flaked out on the other bed rather than return to his room and looked just as deep in sleep as Mandy.

She threw her purse on the chair and headed for the bathroom. She could try to snatch a few winks in a chair, but she decided to have a long, hot bath instead. Maybe it would restore her good humor in time for the Christmas Eve service.

She poured a liberal amount of bath salts under the hot water and let it swirl into a fragrant foam as she undressed. She dipped a toe in to find it almost uncomfortably warm, but she inched her way in slowly and soon was nearly submerged in the hot, bubbly water.

She thought back to the conversation with Tillie about Edward's death. Why had the police accepted the accidental verdict so easily? Was it because the opener had disappeared? You would think that would make them even more suspicious of foul play unless they believed it had really fallen out in the ambulance and just gotten lost. Maybe they did think his death was something more but couldn't act because there was no hard evidence.

Abby wondered how hard they had questioned Sylvia. Was there any way to bring it up without antagonizing her? Edward's death certainly made things easier for her and paved the way to her arranged reconciliation with Kelly, which was what she had wanted all along. Did Woolly and his partner know about the previous death when they questioned Sylvia about Kelly? Of course, they would. Police forces shared files and information, didn't they? Sylvia's presence at two violent deaths surely couldn't escape their notice.

Maybe she should talk to someone else, but who? Certainly not Mona. Would Belinda be of any help? Then her thoughts turned to Jessie. She would be the one to ask. Jessie was in the house the day Edward died. She was so close to Sylvia that she would know how things were between the couple and if anything untoward had happened before the accident.

Abby sat up suddenly in the tub, remembering the time Jessie had greeted Woolly and his partner. She wanted to get another look at the reception area, and now would be a good time. Everything would be deserted—no arrivals or departures, no bookings. Even the sparse staff left wouldn't be working now.

She nearly slipped jumping out of the tub but towelled off and got dressed in record time. She hesitated with her hand on the door handle and went back to the desk to scribble a quick note to Mandy in case she woke up and wondered at her absence. *Back in fifteen minutes*, she wrote and set it on the edge of the bed where her daughter slept.

Chapter
Twenty-Six

She crept out quietly. She didn't really want to explain what she was doing, because she wasn't sure herself.

As soon as she got downstairs, Abby swivelled her gaze all around the lobby. Not a soul to be seen. The silver and gold Christmas tree twinkled in all its finery. The Christmas music had changed as the important day approached. The silly songs and the modern versions had disappeared to be replaced with a stream of traditional carols that threw out a veil of reverence over the room.

She peeked around the corner of the dining room. It, too, was deserted. Down the hall, only the night lights were on in the gift shop and salon. She took a few steps towards the treatment areas to ensure that was also empty and quiet, lit only by softly colored lights.

The few guests that remained would be in their rooms sharing family time or, like Richard and Mandy, sleeping off the huge dinner and waiting to go to the evening service.

Abby stepped behind the reception desk, trying to bring back the picture of the visit the previous day when Woolly had come up to introduce himself to Jessie. Tonight the computer was shut down, the register door partially open to show it was empty, and the desktop was clear. After another guilty look around, Abby opened the right desk drawer to the maze of pens, pencils, paper clips, and other office equipment that lay in a jumble. On the right side was a long silver letter opener with engraving along the side. It looked sharp compared to the dull, finished one she owned at home. She touched the edge slightly with her thumb and felt the sharp blade. It did look like a dagger. But it was the opener Abby saw Jessie slip into the drawer surreptitiously when she was aware of police presence. She looked closer at the engraving along the handle—the initials S.G. Not Jessie's initials. S could stand for Sylvia. If so, it must have dated back to the days before her marriage, as it didn't match her current initials. If it were a family heirloom, it could go back generations to the original owner.

Abby felt a sudden chill between her shoulder blades and quickly shoved the opener back into the desk. She looked around but couldn't see any sign of life. Her imagination was running wild, thinking someone had been watching her. She shook off the feeling as she carefully moved to the other side of the desk. She didn't want Mona to catch her snooping into drawers, or they would all be out on their ears.

She stood, for a moment, pondering her next move. She could go upstairs and see if Mandy or Richard were awake yet. Nothing in the spa was open, and even Tillie had left for the night. She took a few steps down the hallway, past the dining room and into the corridor that led to the treatment area. The door was closed and locked, but, because the stairway inside led up to the twenty-four hour exercise room, any guest room key could open it. Abby slid hers in and slipped to the other side. She could always say she was looking for the treadmills if she were asked what she was doing there. The little anteroom was locked. Of course, it would be. There were supplies and products for sale in that room. Why hadn't it been locked the night Kelly was killed? She imagined Sylvia had left it open deliberately. Or, maybe she had been sure to get there first in order to unlock it. Yes, she had said she arrived before Kelly. The steps going down to the aqua treatment area had a half-door barricade with a chain holding a closed sign. Not much of a deterrent to someone who really wanted in, but then the jets and water could only be turned on with an employee key, so why would anyone want to enter?

Abby did. She wanted to see the whirlpool where Kelly had died. She climbed over the door, nearly losing her balance as she did so. The lights were dimmed with only small night-lights shining along the stairwell by the steps. This was what it would have looked like the night someone dragged Kelly's unconscious body down the stairs to the whirlpool.

The area smelled damp and earthy. A residual scent of essential oils hung in the air from their last use. Abby quickly looked over her shoulder, feeling again that laser on her back. She walked the circle around the waterfalls, the sauna, the glacier shower and the seaweed bath. The whirlpool was one of the last features, and now it sat in the dim light, covered with a tarpaulin. Had the tarp been there the night Kelly had died? Had it been removed by the killer? Or had it recently been added as a safety feature?

Stone shelves protruded from the walls with spots to put water glasses or towels. The one closest to the whirlpool was where Kelly's clothes had been left in a pile. The killer must have thought, if Kelly were found naked in the pool, it would be assumed she had gotten in the whirlpool of her own free will, undressing quickly for a spontaneous dip. The scene was definitely planned to look like an accident. They wouldn't know that, in life, Kelly was a neat freak and would never have left her clothes in that disorderly heap.

Abby felt, rather than saw, a movement behind her. Before she could turn, she felt the blow to her head, and the lights went out.

Chapter Twenty-Seven

When she came to, she was lying on a hard surface, her head throbbing wildly. She opened her eyes with difficulty, staring into another set of eyes that were glaring back at her in anger. She tried to move, but her hands were behind her back, held immobile by what felt like tape of some kind. She opened her mouth to speak, but something silver flashed towards her throat. Jessie was holding the dagger-like opener against her neck.

"No talking," she said in a whisper. She jerked Abby to her feet and pointed to the sliding partition in front of them. "In there," Jessie said as she shoved Abby into the sauna stall.

Abby's legs were unsteady. She half-fell, half-sat on the bench inside.

Jessie shut the door behind them and sat facing her. "You just didn't know when to stop poking around, did you?"

"All I did..."

"Shut up. I'm doing the talking." Jessie spoke in a low voice, not intended to carry. How close would the nearest set of ears be? If Abby yelled, would someone come to help before Jessie was able to use that lethal looking opener? There was no certainty anyone would be there to hear, so Abby decided to follow the prudent course of doing as she was told and hoping for a chance to bolt.

She decided to match Jessie's low tones. "It was you who dragged Kelly down the stairs to the whirlpool?" Abby hoped Jessie would want to talk about what she had done. It must have been hard to keep it all in, not able to talk to anyone. Now she would get the chance to talk, expecting Abby would never be able to tell anyone what she knew. Abby hoped to prove her wrong about the last part.

"Of course. I didn't want to hurt Kelly. It was all a huge mistake."

"A mistake? How?"

"I saw Gran leave her room, and I knew something was up. I followed her to be sure she wasn't in any kind of trouble. I overheard their conversation. Then, when she ran out, I looked in and saw Kelly on the floor. I thought she was dead. I knew Gran would tell Mona, and she'd get into a lot of trouble, so I decided to move Kelly and make it look as though she had an accident in the whirlpool."

"When did Kelly come to?"

"When I finished undressing her and put her in the water, she opened her eyes. I nearly jumped out of my skin. I had to shut her up, so I pushed her head under the water and held her there till she stopped moving."

"You could have called for help. Then she would still be alive, and she would tell everyone she fell. Sylvia wouldn't have been in any trouble at all."

"But then she'd tell them how I moved her and tried to kill her. No, I had to finish her." Jessie clutched the dagger a little tighter, and Abby flinched as it scraped her skin. She tried to pull away, but Jessie held her hair with her other hand and pulled it tightly.

"Now, I'll have to look after you, too."

"How in the world will you make this look like an accident? You'll have blood all over you. They'll find traces of it."

Jessie looked at her with scornful eyes. "I'm not going to stab you." Then she added, "Unless you make me, that is. No, you're going to have an accident as well. I'm sorry the spa is going to have a bad reputation after this, but I don't really care about Mona's troubles as long as Gran is safe. You are going to die in the sauna. Too much heat for too long and you'll pass out and have a heart attack. No one will think twice about it. You're getting on after all and a little overweight."

Abby flushed at the characterization, but it seemed minor compared to her other woes.

"You were watching me at the reception desk," said Abby. The longer she could keep Jessie talking, the better chance she had of getting someone's attention. If only she had woken Mandy or Richard before she'd left. Would they find her note? Would they be awake yet? She wondered how long it would take them to start worrying and come looking for her.

"I saw you look in the desk. I saw you pick up the dagger. I knew then that you had figured out what happened to Edward."

"You killed him, didn't you?"

"Of course. He was always so mean to Gran. That day, they had a terrible fight. She was crying and so unhappy, and I was the only one who could protect her from him. Mona wouldn't do anything. Belinda had no idea how bad things were. It was up to me."

"How did you arrange his accident?"

"Those old stairs were terrible. They were way too steep and the carpet at the top was worn. Gran nearly fell down them the week before. So I pulled at the tear in the carpet on the landing to make it a little worse. Then, when Uncle Edward came down the stairs, he caught his toe. It wouldn't have mattered if he hadn't. I'm young and strong, and he wouldn't have been able to see me behind him in time. When he stumbled, I just slipped up behind him and pushed him down the stairs."

"He fell on the opener?"

"He was supposed to break his neck falling down the stairs, but he was too miserable to make it easy for me. He already had the letters in his hand when he fell. I ran down after him, and he was still alive. He opened his eyes and looked right at me. So I ran to get the opener, and I put his hand around it and pushed hard. Then I ran away and called for the ambulance."

"Why did you go back to get the opener? Weren't you afraid that would make it look like someone arranged the accident?"

"I couldn't let it go with the police. That dagger was given to Gran by her grandfather. It's old as the hills. It really was a dagger, you see. She only used it for an opener. Then she told me I could have it. It was a gift from her, so I couldn't let them take it away."

As Jessie rambled on about how easily and without re-morse she had killed two people, Abby's stomach leaped around as though it were trying to leave her body. If she couldn't think of some distraction soon, if no one came to look for her... Abby tried to focus. She had to think about escape rather than the consequences if she didn't. Never to see Man-dy and Matthew again, never to see her yet-to-be grandchil-dren... *Stop it!* She tried to concentrate on Jessie's words. The longer she talked, the more chance Abby had to get away.

"The lighter," she said as Jessie seemed to be winding down. "What made you think of the lighter?" Abby pulled and twisted at her bound wrists as unobtrusively as she could, but the tape only seemed to tighten as she moved.

"It was in lost and found. Someone found it in the dining room and dropped it off. It had your ex's initials on it, and I'd seen him with a gold lighter earlier, so I knew it was his. It was the perfect way to throw suspicion on someone else if they didn't believe the accident part. It was so easy. When I went looking for Kelly the next morning, I took the lighter with me and dropped it beside the pool before coming back to yell, 'Call an ambulance.'" Jessie took the dagger away to use her hand to make an accompanying gesture to her tale, but it still gave Abby no window to escape. Jessie's other hand held her head in a vice-like grip, and the dagger imme-diately returned to her throat.

"What are you going to do now?" As soon as she spoke the words, Abby cursed herself. She should be trying to keep the story going, not nudging Jessie on to her next move.

"I'm going to lock you in the sauna, turn up the heat and wait for you to die. You will, you know. We have all those safety lectures about overstaying in the sauna. If you stay too long, your blood pressure drops, you get dehydrated, and eventually your heart just stops. Everyone will believe you were just being stupid after a drink or two, and you will suffer such a tragic death. They'll say someone of your age should have known better, then shrug it off and forget all about you."

"No one is going to think I came in here fully dressed." If Jessie had to take off her wrist bindings to undress her, she might stand a chance.

"I'll undress you after, and put you in a robe. Then I'll

quit this place and leave Mona to deal with it all. I'm going to take Gran away somewhere. She still has lots of Uncle Edward's money. We'll go somewhere warm and buy a little place, and I'll take care of her. She needs someone to take care of her, like she always took care of me when I was little. She's the only one who ever really loved me." Jessie's eyes misted over a little as she talked, but only for a moment. Then her face hardened again, and she produced a roll of tape from her pocket, presumably the same tape that was on Abby's wrists.

Abby had to act soon. Even if she couldn't make it out of the reach of that dagger, she had to try. At least Jessie would be caught if she had to stab her. Richard would be free, and Mandy and Matthew would have their father. She heard a strange sound and quickly looked up at Jessie before realizing the strangled sob had come from her. She couldn't hold back another muffled cry, but she had to stop. She had to do something to change the course of Jessie's plan, to make her rethink and re-plan.

Chapter
Twenty-Eight

Jessie set down the dagger for a moment, far away from Abby's reach—even if her hands weren't tied—to tear a strip of tape from the roll. Abby seized the moment and lunged at her the best she could with her hands behind her. She yelled loudly as she did and was amazed to see Jessie actually fall to the floor, caught by surprise. Abby stood unsteadily and pushed with her shoulder at the door. But the younger and unfettered Jessie was able to move more quickly. She was upright in seconds and grabbed Abby away from the door, but not before Abby heard a clatter at the top of the stairs— the sound of the chain being moved. Someone was coming. She opened her mouth to give another scream, but a hand firmly clamped it shut.

She hoped Jessie hadn't heard the same sound she had. She knew Jessie would do all she could to avoid killing Abby with the dagger. It wasn't part of her plan. She would never have her life with Sylvia if she were caught.

She bit down on the hand across her mouth, not hard enough to do damage, but it was enough to make Jessie pull her hand away long enough for Abby to let out one more scream.

It was all she needed. The door burst open, not to Richard or Mandy as she'd expected, but to Mona and Sylvia.

Jessie stared at the newcomers and dropped the dagger

in utter surprise.

"Gran! What are you doing here?"

"Jessie, what have you done?" The words came from Sylvia in a sort of wail, and Jessie threw herself into her arms, paying no attention to Abby or Mona. Her great-aunt was her whole world, the only one that mattered to her.

Mona reached for the dagger till Abby let out a whispered, "Better not touch it."

Mona looked at her and nodded. She ushered Abby into the corridor and motioned to her mother to come along with the now sobbing Jessie.

When they reached the top of the stairs, Mona took out her phone and made the emergency call before finding a pair of scissors in the anteroom desk to cut Abby free from her tape. They trooped down the hall together, a strange procession, to the reception area.

Mandy and Richard were coming down the stairs and stopped in the middle of a step as though caught in slow motion. If the situation hadn't been so serious, Abby would have laughed at the startled expressions they wore. Then Mandy moved, running down the remaining stairs to take Abby in her arms. Richard was right behind her.

"We woke up and you weren't there," said Mandy. "Then we found your note and were afraid you were off getting into trouble."

"And we were right," Richard grinned.

They all glanced over to the family group who stood beside the reception desk. Jessie seemed to have lost all her energy and hatred. She allowed Sylvia to lead her into the office, deflated like a pricked balloon. Mona was on the phone again, and they heard her talking to Theo, ordering him to come down and stand guard at the treatment area to be sure no one entered.

She set down the phone and turned to Abby. "I suppose you think I owe you an apology." Before Abby could answer, she went on. "Well, you're not going to get it. If you hadn't meddled, you never would have been in danger. Jessie was only trying to protect Mother."

"She killed Kelly!" cried Abby. "You can't find any way to blame Kelly for her own death, can you? And what about your father? Did you know she killed him, too?"

Mona appeared to consider before answering. "Well,

maybe a small apology then. I'm sorry. I'm sorry to you as well." She looked at Richard. "We all really thought you had done it. We didn't know Jessie was responsible. Honestly."

"Did you never suspect your father's death was something other than an accident?"

"I did wonder a little at the time, but the police didn't pursue it, so I took it as an accident." Mona bit down on her lip. "I even thought for a moment that maybe Mother..." Her voice trailed off. "I know father was a bit difficult sometimes if you didn't know how to handle him, but he wasn't really a bad person. He merely had problems with people who wouldn't stand up for themselves. If mother had learned to stand up to him when they were first married, I'm sure things would have been totally different."

She looked into the office where her mother was holding a still sobbing Jessie who didn't look as though she was about to run out of tears any time soon.

"You're lucky Mother and I came downstairs tonight to get a snack. I saw a light on in the corridor where there shouldn't be one. Then, when I went to check, I heard a yell and, well, you're just lucky. That's all."

Mona turned her gaze to the office and went on. "If I had thought Jessie had anything to do with it, I would have done something. I really would have. I never suspected for a moment, though I did realize her attachment to Mother was a little over the top."

A couple of spa guests wandered out of the elevator, and Mona commanded more damage control. She said to Abby, "You and your family might as well go to your rooms. I'll call you when the police want to talk to you."

Abby was about to protest, still unwilling to trust the account Mona might give to them, but her daughter and ex-husband outvoted her. Each taking one arm, they ushered her upstairs. Abby took a quick look over her shoulder and saw Mona talking to the couple, already back in her hostess role, keeping things quiet and putting on a good face.

She felt suddenly tired and was happy to let herself be taken upstairs.

Chapter Twenty-Nine

When they got to the room, her family turned to face her. "You're not going to get a chance to rest until you tell us everything," said Mandy.

Abby sighed melodramatically, but knew she would be quite happy to unburden herself and tell the whole story. It still felt like a dream, like something that had happened to another person. But she knew she would soon fully realize how close she had come to death, and then the shock and fear would set in.

Now, she shrugged and said, "You get the whole story in return for a very large glass of wine." She waited till it was produced and took a long sip, savoring the normalcy of the action and of the scene around her. Then she stretched out on the bed and began to tell her tale.

She had nearly finished bringing them up-to-date when the phone rang. It was Belinda, asking her to come down and talk to the police. Belinda must have been summoned by Mona after Abby left. Mona did believe in keeping up a united family front. The way she kept a close finger on all the activities of her family members made Abby wonder again if she was as unknowing as she said she was about the events surrounding Edward's and Kelly's deaths.

Woolly and his sidekick were waiting for her, all business with no apologies on their part for their earlier erroneous suspicions. Abby couldn't help giving Woolly a glare to let him know she hadn't forgotten. She hadn't yet forgiven him for the Miss Marple reference either.

"Before we begin, let me tell you we take a dim view of people trying to insert themselves into an investigation. You could have been killed. You should have left things to us."

Abby's anger flared in spite of her intense sense of weariness. "You had the wrong person. I couldn't let you get it all wrong, not when my family was involved." For a second, she wondered if she were as bad as Mona with her emphasis on family solidarity.

"We would have come to the right conclusions eventually," said Woolly. "We have to do things in a methodical way in the police investigation, following all leads and ruling things out before coming to the final conclusion. You jumped right in without knowing anything and could have jeopardized the whole investigation."

Abby was too tired to argue, so she let it slide.

When she finished with the interview, she looked at her watch. It seemed like midnight and Christmas already, but it was still evening. In spite of the end of a difficult situation, she didn't feel the least bit festive. She only felt tired, so tired she thought she could sleep for a week. Which was just what she intended to do. She would bypass the evening lunch and the midnight service in favor of sleep.

When she trudged through the doorway to the room, it was in semi-darkness. Richard was no longer there, and Mandy was lying in bed, head bundled up against a pile of pillows waiting for her.

"Are you all finished with the police?" she asked.

"For now. I'm sure there will be more questions later."

"I nearly fell asleep waiting for you. I'm still full of turkey. Do you want to go down for something to eat?"

"No, that huge turkey dinner has me set till morning. I don't have the energy to go down anyhow. Are you still planning to go to the evening service? I'm going to take a pass, if you don't mind."

"Me, too. Dad and I already talked about it. He's going to make a few phone calls and have an early night. I thought maybe we could just lie in bed, turn on the TV to catch one more round of *It's a Wonderful Life,* and doze off. I'll even take the remote so you can go to sleep whenever you want."

"Sounds like a plan to me. I intend to be out like a light long before Clarence gets his wings."

Chapter Thirty

Christmas Day began late for Abby. She had slept through the night, a rare occurrence for her. The sun was already shining which meant, at this time of the year, she had really slept in.

There was no sign of Mandy, although the coffee carafe was half-full of fresh coffee, so she couldn't be long gone. Abby filled her cup and stood looking out the window. What she saw was pristine perfection, a far cry from the events that had happened here this week. She looked around the room and thought she couldn't get out of here quickly enough. She was dying to get home to her own familiar surroundings, to Ajax, and to a phone conversation with Matthew.

She was just slipping into a hot tub when she heard the sound of the door opening.

"Breakfast is served when you're ready, or would you like it in the bath?" called Mandy from the other room.

"If you have a refill on the coffee, I'll take it in here." Abby pulled the shower curtain nearly closed and smelled the lovely aroma of an unhealthy breakfast. Bacon and scrambled eggs and even a croissant were on the plate, topped off by a steaming carafe of coffee. Mandy set the dishes down beside the tub and took a seat on the toilet.

"Thank you, Mandy. You've made my day, and it's only eight o'clock."

"I thought you might not want to sit in the dining room this morning. Not that there's anyone there. Only one woman was dishing up the buffet. No sign of a Davenport anywhere," Mandy said from the other side of the shower curtain. "I'll leave you in peace. I'm going to start packing. Dad is talking to the police this morning along with his lawyer to be sure he can go home, and I can't wait to get out of here."

"I hear you," said Abby. "I don't think I'll be staying in a spa any time soon. I guess we'd better go online to book our flights home."

"All taken care of," said Mandy.

"You have us all booked back to Winnipeg? Are we on the same flight? I guess the holiday bookings will be slowing down now that Christmas has actually arrived."

"Not exactly," said Mandy.

"Oh well, I guess on holiday time you have to take what you can get."

"We have a little surprise for you." Abby could hear Mandy grinning.

"What?"

"Well, you aren't coming with us. I made a call to Neil. Sorry, I snooped on your cell phone this morning while you were still sleeping to get his number. He's going to be there for another four days, and you are on your way to join him."

"Mandy! You are wonderful. You got all that accomplished while I was still snoring?"

"Yep."

"I owe you some money for the booking. I know you don't have much to spare, so I'll stop and get some cash for you."

Mandy interrupted. "It's Dad's treat. He told me to put it on his credit card. He says he owes you that much and more."

You're right about the more, thought Abby to herself, but she wasn't about to look a gift horse in the mouth. Not when it was flying her to Turks and Caicos and to Neil.

She sank back into the tub. There was nothing like the vision of sun, sand, and sea to make you forget you nearly died in a sauna only hours ago.

"There's only one thing missing to make our departure complete," she said.

"What?" asked Mandy. "You surely don't want to book a mud treatment or a massage with the delicious Theo?"

"No," said Abby with an impish smile. "But I never had a chance to get my free reading from Belinda. Now, I will always wonder what my aura looks like."

About the Author

Sharon McGregor is a prairie transplant now living on the west coast. Her imagination and story weaving got its start when she was an only child living on a farm. She's moved on from cowgirl dreams to romance and mystery, but hasn't lost her love for horses. When she can summon up the nerve to get on a plane, she's terrified of flying like Abby, she likes to visit with her son and grandchildren who are still knee deep in the prairies.

Sharon loves endings with resolutions, which is why she enjoys writing cozy mysteries. She has an ongoing fight with her cat Zoey for control of the computer keyboard. Murder at The Island Spa is the second book in the Island series